The Company of The Silver Hare

Joy Pitt

For Niamh
with love.x.x

The Company of The Silver Hare

by

Joy Pitt

The Company of The Silver Hare

Text copyright©2019 Joy Pitt
Cover design and artwork©2019 Joy Pitt

ISBN 978-1-908577-87-0

First Published in Great Britain
1 3 5 4 2

British Library Cataloguing in Publication Data.
A catalogue record for this book is available from the British Library.

Printed and bound in Great Britain by CPI Group (UK) Ltd.
Croydon CR0 4YY

Hawkwood Books 2019

To the memory of my Grandad,
Edward Henry Pitt, 1898-1987.
The best storyteller I've ever known.

1. SPOTS AND HOW TO CURE THEM

Emmet lay on his tummy in the long grass at the top of Pendle Hill. He had a twig in his grubby hand and he was poking an ant's nest with it, watching as they scurried helter-skelter in all directions. He had tears running down his face and, every now and then, one would plop onto the ground amongst the bewildered ants. In the distance he could hear the voices of the twins, Hetty and Letty. They were chanting loudly, "Emmet has a spot face, Emmet has a spot face, spotty Emmet, spotty Emmet!"

Emmet lifted his head slightly and peered down the hill at his tormentors, two skinny, scruffy yellow headed girls of seven years old, his younger sisters. They had hazel switches in their hands and were swishing at the long grass, searching for him.

He flattened himself down and lay quiet. With any luck they wouldn't find him – this time. They were heading in the wrong direction. The chanting had stopped. He raised his head again. The twins had disturbed a cloud of butterflies which rose from the hillside. The girls forgot their brother, threw down their switches and began to chase the butterflies down the hill, whooping and leaping in delight.

Emmet stopped crying and sniffed hard. He didn't sit up until he could no longer hear them. He blew his nose on his grimy sleeve. He did indeed have spots. He was twelve years old, and a big boy for his age, tall and slightly plump. Teenage spots had come early to Emmet, great red angry ones that formed yellow pustules and were sore. Emmet couldn't leave them alone, and the twins, who loved to tease their brother, wouldn't leave *him* alone.

He got up and wandered over to the stone cross next to the holy well and sat himself down, moodily, setting his chin on his knees. His mother had tried many cures to get rid of the spots. Leeches was one, and he shuddered at the memory. She was threatening to get the barber to let his blood, and Emmet was terrified at the thought. His father once had to have his blood let, and Emmet had felt sweaty and dizzy at the sight. He had gone outside and been sick in his mother's herb patch. His mother had walloped him for that, and the twins had laughed. They didn't mind blood and had found the bloodletting rather interesting.

"I can get rid of your spots," said a quiet voice in his ear.

Emmet jumped and banged his head on the stone. He had thought he was alone on the hillside. Standing in front of him was a girl, about his own age but small and finely made. She had long, wild red hair and her eyes were emerald green. He was so surprised to see her there that his mouth hung open stupidly for a moment.

"Close your mouth," she said saucily, "the flies will get in."

With an effort, Emmet closed his mouth and pulled himself together.

"You're Jennet," he said. "You're the…" he tailed off, but she seemed to read his thoughts.

"The witch's child, that's what you were going to say, weren't you?"

Emmet looked at his feet. He felt uncomfortable. That was precisely what he had been about to say, but it seemed rude, and besides, next to the pretty, smooth faced Jennet he felt as though his spots were as red and shining as a sunset over Pendle Hill. Jennet sat down next to him.

"I can, you know," she said affably. "It's easy."

Emmet said, "No bloodletting?"

"No bloodletting."

"No leeches?"

"No leeches."

"Are you going to cast a spell on me?" asked Emmet. His face puckered into a worried frown. "My mother will be furious."

"Your mother won't know," said Jennet. "And she'll be glad when your spots go away and she doesn't have to pay the barber."

2

This was so undoubtedly true that Emmet couldn't argue with it.

"Well, alright," he said, "but what will you do? And will it hurt?" he added.

Before Jennet could answer, the sound of the twins' voices floated up to them on the warm summer breeze. They were running uphill towards them, joined by a small, plump girl of around five, the youngest sister of the family. She was much out of breath and protesting loudly as the twins dragged her between them, each hauling a chubby arm.

"Ow, let go, you're hurting my arms. I can't go so fast, I'm not big yet."

The twins let go and the girl, not ready, fell flat on her face in the long grass and immediately set up a loud wail. Emmet stood up, strode the few paces towards the howling child and lifted her up.

"Come on, Lily, you're all right. Look, no scrape, let me rub it for you."

He set her on her feet and rubbed her knees, then took her small hand and led her up to the others.

The twins were staring curiously at Jennet.

"Are you..?" they asked together.

"Yes, I am," said Jennet defiantly. "And I'm going to cure your brother's spots for him."

"These are my sisters," said Emmet, shyly. "Hetty and Letty are the twins, and this one is Lily. I'm Emmet."

Lily had been staring at Jennet with her thumb in her mouth. She took it out with a loud pop.

"You're the witch's child," she said. "Witches are bad, everyone in the village says. Does that mean you're bad too?"

Emmet was mortified at her outspokenness. Jennet's green eyes crinkled, and Emmet couldn't help thinking again how pretty she was.

"There's good witches and there's bad witches," she said. "Same as there's good people and bad people. Do you think it would be bad to take Emmet's spots away?"

Lily shook her head, her thumb still firmly stuck in her

3

mouth.

"I think it would be a good thing," said Letty.

"Emmet's spots make us feel sick." This was Hetty.

"Spotty face, spotty face, Emmet's got a spotty face."

"Shut up," Emmet hissed.

Lily took out her thumb again.

"What's it like being a witch?" she asked. Jennet's pretty face clouded.

"Lonely," she said. "No one wants to play with me. It would be nice to have some friends."

"Haven't you got a brother?" asked Emmet. "I've seen you with a boy."

Jennet looked down at her bare feet.

"That's Jimmy," she said, "but he isn't like other people. He's not quite right. Ma says he was moonstruck when he was born. He can't talk much, and he can't learn like other people. But he's good," she said, defensively. "He's kind and we all love him." She glanced down the hill. "Here he comes, now."

A small figure was meandering up towards them. Although obviously older than the children, he was short and round with a waddling walk, and his eyes were pixie-like. Under his arm he carried a large brown hen.

"My Jennet," he said happily, in a voice which wasn't clear. He came up to his sister and gave her a one-armed hug, the other arm clutched tight around his hen. Jennet hugged him back and gave him a kiss. The twins stared. Jimmy certainly was odd looking, and as for Jennet kissing him, well, they never kissed their brother, most certainly not since he developed spots. The thought of kissing spotty Emmet made them giggle, and Jennet, misinterpreting the laughter, glared at them.

"Don't laugh at him," she said angrily, "you'll hurt his feelings, and it's mean."

"We weren't," said Letty, hastily, "truly we weren't."

Jimmy sat himself down on the grass in one swift movement, an amazing feat of agility for one so clumsy looking, and sat with his legs folded under him, like an

4

acrobat. He still clutched the hen which looked at the children beadily. Lily surprised everyone by going over to Jimmy and smiling. She plumped herself down next to him.

"I can cross my legs too," she said. "Not as good as you though, that's 'cos I'm not big yet."

She stretched out a small, grubby hand and stroked the hen.

"I like your chicky. What's her name?"

"My Henny Penny," Jimmy grinned back at her. He seemed to have quite a few teeth missing, and his tongue was large and thick. "Who your name?"

"I'm Lily," said Lily, "and this is Hetty and this is Letty and this is Emmet."

Jimmy put out his hand and gently touched one of Lily's curls. "My Lily. I like you, Lily."

The hen squawked loudly and struggled in Jimmy's arms.

"Put her down, Jimmy," said Jennet, gently. "Look, she wants to get down. Let her have a peck about."

Jimmy put down the chicken which shook out its glossy brown feathers and began to peck at the ground. The children sat down, making a rough circle with Lily and Jimmy. No one said anything for a moment. The air was alive, yet drowsy with the hum of insects. In the blue sky were fluffy, white clouds, moving gently with the light wind. Emmet, gazing upwards felt as though Pendle Hill was the centre of the world, with everything else spinning away from its axis. He also had the strangest sense that something had begun.

"How will you cure Emmet's spots, Jennet?" asked Letty.

"She'll make a potion," said Hetty. "It will be smelly and stinky and have toads in it, all boiled and horrible, and horse manure and dog poo and spotty Emmet will have to drink it and it will take away his spots, but he'll fall down dead – like this!"

Hetty threw herself on the ground, rolled her eyes upwards, and let her tongue loll out of the side of her mouth. Both the twins went off into peals of wicked laughter and rolled about, kicking their dirty, bare legs in the air.

"I shall make a potion," said Jennet, "but it will be as sweet as roses. You must meet me here at midnight on the night of the full moon and I will show you how to use it."

"That's tomorrow," said Emmet. "The full moon is tomorrow."

"It is," said Jennet. "Meet me here at moonrise and we shall see what we shall see. Come on, Jimmy. It's almost suppertime. Bring Henny Penny. See? She's laid an egg."

Jimmy got to his feet and tucked the brown hen under his arm. He picked up the egg with gentle fingers.

"Egg for my Lily." Jimmy laid it in her chubby hand. "Special egg," he added.

He put his free hand into the hand of Jennet and without saying goodbye, the witch's children began to run down the hill. The hen, jiggling up and down under Jimmy's arm, gave an indignant squawk. Emmet and his sisters stared after them, then turned and examined the still-warm egg.

"Why is it special, Emmet?" Lily wanted to know.

"I'm not sure, Lily." Emmet took the egg from her hand and turned it round. It looked like a perfectly ordinary hen's egg. "You could have it for your tea, if you like," he said.

"No." Lily was decided. "It's a special egg, Jimmy said so. I shall save it til I'm big."

Being big was a state towards which Lily longingly aspired. Emmet, Hetty and Letty were big, in her eyes. When she was big, all things would be possible, but exactly when this magical bigness would be conferred upon her, she wasn't sure. Possibly when she was six, Lily thought, but as she had only just celebrated her fifth birthday, being six seemed far away in the distant future.

"Oh, Lily," said Hetty gently. The twins were fond of their small sister. "If you save it 'til you're big, it will go bad."

"Have it for your tea," advised Letty. "Ma will cook it for you."

Lily was obstinate. "I'm going to save it. It's my special egg and no one can eat it."

"Alright Lily." Emmet knew his sister. "Let's find you

something to carry it home in."

The twins looked about and found some moss. Lily herself spied an old bird's nest, low down in the hedge. Emmet wrapped the still warm egg in the moss and laid it carefully in the old nest.

"Shall I carry it for you? If you fall over, it might get broken and you'd be sad."

Lily's bottom lip began to protrude, and a mutinous look spread over her face.

"It's my egg and I'm carrying it."

Emmet sighed in resignation. "Come on then, you carry your egg and I'll carry you, how's that?"

Lily nodded, grudgingly. Emmet bent down and the twins lifted her onto his shoulders. They set off down the hill to Barley village where their father kept the forge. He was a great, tall, thick-set fellow, red in the face from his long hours labouring over the furnace. Despite his somewhat alarming appearance, he was as mild and gentle as a lamb. He sat now, on a stool outside the forge, his day's work done, smoking a clay pipe of tobacco.

"Now, you young 'uns," he said, the pipe still clamped between his teeth, "where have you been? Your Ma's been calling for you all. Supper's ready and it's rabbit stew."

The blacksmith's forge was a low-stone building which held a fascination for all the village children. It was particularly beloved by them in winter as it was always warm. It also housed the village bread oven. The two up, two down cottage where the family lived was joined onto the forge, and that was warm too. On a hot summer's day, it was a trifle too warm, and Ma emerged from the cottage door, red in the face from cooking.

"Wash your hands, quick now." She pushed wisps of hair back from her sweaty forehead. "There's water in the bucket by the door. We'll sup outside tonight, it's such a fine evening. You're all filthy. Where have you been? Lily, what's that in your hand?"

Emmet and the twins exchanged anxious glances but Lily

7

beamed at her mother. "My special egg," she announced, proudly. "Henny Penny laid it and Jimmy said I could have it."

Her mother looked puzzled. "Jimmy, who's Jimmy? I don't know of any Jimmy."

Pa had an amused look on his face. "Old Demdike's grandson, that's who she means. Him they say is moonstruck. Goes around with a hen under his arm. No harm in him."

"Jennet's a witch," said Lily, "but I think she's a good witch, Pa. She's going to cure Emmet's spots. And she's pretty. Witches aren't pretty are they, Pa?"

"Old Demdike is a Cunning Woman," said her father. "Witch is a strong word to use. Trouble comes to folk that use that word. You remember that, young Lily. Jennet's a Cunning Woman like her Ma and Gran, and if she can cure Emmet's spots, that will be a fine thing."

Ma had a strange look on her face. "Be careful who you make friends with, that's all, and guard your egg well. A special egg, now there's a thing."

There was something not being said, Emmet felt. Some feeling, like a crackling in the air, like summer lightning, and a glance exchanged between his Ma and Pa – was that a ghost of a wink?

"Come now," said Ma, "stew's ready, like I said. Hetty and Letty, help with the dishing up. Lily, fetch the bread. Emmet, bring the spoons."

Soon the family was enjoying their supper, Emmet and his parents on stools and the girls in a row on the doorstep. They ate with horn spoons, precious, carefully wiped and laid away in the cupboard when not in use. Afterwards, the girls had to help their mother wash the dishes and sweep the floor whilst Emmet and his father tidied the forge.

"St. John's Eve, tomorrow," remarked Pa, hanging up his enormous bellows. "Midsummer's Eve and a full moon at that. A magical time, young Emmet. The little people will be out and about for sure. The longest day of the year. Not always it falls on a full moon. All kinds of wonders can happen at such a time. Be prepared, my son, that's all I say. Be prepared."

8

2. THE BEE MISTRESS

The next day dawned bright and sunny. In the morning Emmet had to help his father in the forge. He was learning how to be a blacksmith, in readiness to take over from him one day. The sign over the forge already read 'W. Smith & Sons'. Sadly, Emmet was the only son. Three previous boys, Charlie, Will and John, and two girls, Rosie and Janie, lay buried in the peace of the churchyard, all dead of diphtheria. Sometimes on a Sunday after church, the girls and Ma would lay posies on the weathered stone which marked their graves. Emmet could just remember them, but they had died seven years ago when he was three, so it was hard to feel sad, although he knew his Ma still did, for she shed tears when she tended the little graves. The twins had been born just after the epidemic, and Lily two years after that, but the lost brothers and sisters were real to them. Lily thought of them still as living people, talked to them and took them presents.

"Look Charlie, a magpie's feather," she would say. "John and Will, here's an apple – you can share it, and Rosie and Janie, here's a stone with a hole in it. You can take it in turns."

She would leave her offering on the graves and they had always gone by the next visit. The twins half-believed in ghosts, climbing out at night to claim their gifts, and Lily was certain of it, but Emmet, not convinced, suspected his father of playing along with Lily's game.

The girls had to work with their mother, milking the family's goat, making cheese and working in the garden behind the cottage and the forge, churning butter. Ma also made fine lace which she wrapped in rough cloth to keep it clean and sold to the gentry, whenever she had a good length finished.

After their lunch of potage and sallet from the garden, Ma announced her intention of visiting Mistress Alice of Roughlee Hall. She put on a clean linen bonnet, scrubbed the girls' faces, and bid them tidy themselves up. She looked at Emmet's spots, sighed, and shook her head.

"Straighten your hair, son," she said. "It's the best we can do with you until young Jennet works her charm."

Emmet flushed under the hated spots and bit his lip. The family owned no looking glass, but he needed no mirror to know just how awful they must appear. If only Jennet could cure him!

"I've some lace for my lady and she has promised me some honey from her bees," went on Ma. "I've some saffron for her, picked today, the most potent time of summer. It's good for the heart and good for the stomach."

She picked up her basket and sallied forth, Emmet and the girls skipping at her side. Neighbours stopped to greet them and doff their hats, for the Smith family was well regarded in the area. Lily still clutched the bird's nest containing her 'special egg'. Her mother had found her a small linen bag to carry it in as she flatly refused to be parted from it. She waved royally to everyone she passed, and all smiled at the funny little girl, a great favourite with the villagers.

"Not big yet, young Lily?" asked an old man, with a sly grin, as they passed his garden.

"Not yet," Lily said. "Soon I 'spect I will be."

They made their way to the end of the village and crossed the bridge over Pendle Water. Their way led them across meadowland studded with bright flowers and waving grasses. As they strolled along, a man came galloping towards them, forcing them to step aside. Mistress Smith dropped a curtsey but the man did not acknowledge her greeting and the horses hooves thundered over the turf creating a great cloud of dust, so close that Lily hid her face in her mother's skirts.

"Master Roger Nowell, magistrate." Ma looked angry. "Fancies himself as gentry. My old goat Bessie has better manners."

Emmet and the twins rubbed gritty dust from their eyes. Hetty had a stubborn speck in hers and her mother took it out with the tip of her own tongue.

Then came the first of many moments which would

change their lives, although it did not seem so at the time. An enormous hare with staring eyes and silvery brown fur shot across the turf. Faster than lightning, faster than any shooting star, it crossed the meadow under the nose of the magistrate's high black horse. Startled, the horse reared up and Roger Nowell was thrown heavily from its back. As Ma and the children watched, he picked himself up, unharmed but furious. He began to chase the horse which was cantering off at a smart pace whilst the hare vanished into a stand of trees. The twins began to giggle helplessly.

"It serves him right, old misery guts," Letty gurgled. "He did look silly."

"I hope he has to chase his horse all the way to Clitheroe," Hetty murmured feelingly. Her eye was still sore.

"Come along," said Ma. "We've still a way to go to Roughlee, and Mistress Alice will be waiting for us."

A figure slipped out of the stand of trees from the exact spot where the hare had disappeared.

"Ma," said Lily, "there is Mistress Alice." She began waving her chubby arm and calling her. The lady crossing the grass towards them was tall and plainly dressed like a countrywoman, although her clothes were of a more expensive quality than those of the children's mother, and the bunch of household keys which hung from her girdle showed that she was a lady of some substance. Her hair under a lace cap was curiously dishevelled.

It was silvery brown in colour.

"Good day, Mistress Smith," said Mistress Alice. She seemed strangely breathless, almost as though she had been running.

"Well met, Mistress Alice," returned their mother, a hint of amusement in her voice. The two women curtsied formally to each other.

"Children," said Ma sharply, "manners, please."

Hastily the three girls bobbed curtsies whilst Emmet ducked his head awkwardly in a semblance of a bow.

"Mistress Alice," began Lily, eagerly, "did you see the

11

hare? It ran right into the trees. Did it bump into you?"

"A hare?" Mistress Alice murmured vaguely. "No Lily, I saw no hare. A pleasant day for a walk, is it not?"

Ma and Alice Nutter exchanged amused glances, and once again Emmet had the curious sensation that more was going on than met the eye.

The two women walked sedately in front of the children, exchanging pleasantries about this and that. Ma, it was whispered in the village, came originally from gentle stock herself, and she was well able to converse like a lady when the occasion arose. The twins and Lily trailed behind, picking daisies and buttercups, whilst Emmet brought up the rear, carrying his mother's basket. They reached Roughlee Hall, a handsome house, looking mellow in the bright afternoon sunshine.

Mistress Alice led them through the pretty gardens filled with herbs and flowers, and a wonderful smell rose up from the lavender and rosemary borders as her skirts brushed them in passing. A table and benches were set out behind the house, surrounded by box hedges, and the scent of roses filled the air. Dotted about the garden were many beehives, looking like straw caps. The tranquil buzzing of foraging bees filled the air.

"Sit you down, Mistress, children," said Mistress Alice. "Would you take a mug of mead and some gingerbread?"

Emmet and the girls nodded enthusiastically.

Mistress Alice disappeared into the cave-like interior of the room behind the back door.

"Anne," they heard her calling, "some refreshments for our guests if you please."

The warm smell of gingerbread wafted out through the open door and the children felt hungry. Mistress Alice returned and seated herself beside Ma.

"I bring you some lace, Mistress, and some saffron, just picked today."

Ma lifted her packages out of the basket and carefully unwrapped the length of lace she had just completed. The delicate pattern stood out starkly white against the rough grain

12

of the oaken table. The twins loved their mother's lace, intricate and delicate as the weaving of spiders. She was beginning to teach them the craft. Each had their own straw cushion and pins, and to while away the winter evenings Pa would whittle bobbins for them. Their fingers didn't yet fly as fast as Ma's, but they'd both made small pieces and were proud of them. Now they leaned one either side of their mother to look at the finished piece.

"Oh Ma," breathed Letty, "it's lovely."

Small Lily climbed up onto the bench so that she could see too.

"Don't touch, Lily," said Ma sharply. "You'll get smudges on it."

Lily's plump finger stopped mid air.

"Wasn't going to," she said with some dignity. "I just wanted to show Mistress Alice the bee..."

"I can see it, Lily," she said. "It's beautiful, and your mother is a clever woman."

Woven into the lace was a picture of a bee, life sized and quite perfect, and as they sat admiring it, a real bee flew over the table, hovered for a moment, then landed on the lace, fitting itself perfectly over the picture.

"Your Majesty."

What an unexpected thing to say! Even stranger, Mistress Alice and Ma bowed their heads to the bee. After a moment's hesitation, the children awkwardly did the same. The bee flew up from the picture and buzzed for a few moments in front of Mistress Alice's face.

"Of course, Your Highness. As you say, the perfect day for it."

The bee buzzed once more and flew away, over the flowers.

Lily's eyes were like saucers. "Was that bee talking to you, Mistress Alice? Why did you call it 'Your Majesty'?"

"She is the Queen," said Mistress Alice, "and, as such, she commands our respect. I am the bee mistress of these hives. To whom would she speak, if not to me?"

13

"What did she say?" asked Hetty, intrigued.

"She says she is much pleased with the Royal Wedding present that I have commissioned from your mother, and that she intends the Royal Wedding to take place tomorrow, on Midsummer's Day. Her practice flights have gone extremely well and she feels more than ready."

"But Mistress Alice," Emmet asked, "how can you understand her?"

"All languages can be understood if one's heart is open," Mistress Alice explained. "And I dearly love my bees."

The door of the house opened and out came a small, kind faced woman bearing a tray of pewter mugs and a platter of still-warm gingerbread. She bobbed a curtsey and set the tray on the table.

"Here we are," she said. "These two are for the Mistresses," and she set a mug each in front of the ladies. "These are for you children. I've watered them down, Mistress Smith."

"Thank you, Anne." said Ma. "They are a little young for full-strength mead just yet."

The children sipped the mead and munched the gingerbread. The mead was made from the bee's honey and Emmet decided that it was like drinking liquid sunshine. For a time, the only sound was of the droning bees, busy all over the garden.

"I believe you've had a visit from Roger Nowell," said Ma.

"Indeed, I have."

"And do I gather that the visit was not a happy one?"

"For Master Nowell, not particularly so," said Mistress Alice, "especially at the end," she added with a smile.

Ma gave a peal of laughter. "Pride goes before a fall, so they do say," she observed, "and he certainly had a fall."

The two women laughed, then Mistress Alice spoke more soberly.

"It is the same as always," she said, and her voice was weary. "He wants my land. He has convinced himself that he

14

has a right to it and will not rest until he is in possession of it."

"Oh, my dear," Ma's voice was gentle, "he is a hard and proud man, not easy to stand against."

They were silent for a while until Mistress Alice spoke more brightly.

"We will not speak of difficulties now. It is St. John's Eve, a night of fires, and feasting – and magic," she said, with a queer air of triumph.

"Indeed," Ma agreed, "and tomorrow is the Royal Wedding."

"Mistress Alice," Lily spoke through her last mouthful of gingerbread. "Do you want to see my special egg?"

Mistress Alice turned to Lily. "Yes, indeed child," she said, "show me."

Lily struggled briefly with the linen bag and pulled out the old nest. Emmet tried to help her, but she pushed him away indignantly and unwrapped her precious egg with great care. To Emmet's surprise, it glowed with a tinge of rainbow colours. He rubbed his eyes. 'It must be the bright sunlight,' he thought to himself. Mistress Alice regarded the egg steadily for a long moment. She and Ma exchanged a brief glance.

"Lily, what a lucky girl you are. This is truly special."

Lily beamed importantly. "Henny Penny laid it for me and Jimmy said I could keep it. He's Jennet's brother, and Jennet's a w… I mean, a Cunning Woman," she said, remembering Pa's warning. "She's going to cure Emmet's spots for him at moonrise tonight by the Holy Well."

Lily, at five, couldn't keep anything to herself. Emmet would rather the whole enterprise had been kept from his mother, especially going to the Holy Well after dark. He was afraid that Ma would forbid him from going, and being a thoughtful boy, tried to obey his parents. However, his mother surprised him.

"The perfect night," she said, "and the perfect time. Old Demdike has taught her well. Just in time for you to look nice for the Royal Wedding, Emmet. It's good that we didn't need to get the barber in. That man is so expensive these days."

"You surely never use that man?" Mistress Alice shook her head disapprovingly. "He's nothing but a butcher."

"Only when appearances need keeping up. You forget, I live in the centre of the village, Mistress."

"Ah, yes," replied Mistress Alice, "it never does to appear too different from one's neighbours, does it?" She leaned confidentially towards the children. "You will accompany your brother on his quest tonight?"

The girls nodded solemnly.

"Then Lily," Mistress Alice was mysterious, "take the special egg with you, won't you? The wheel turns, the young rise and the old must make way. All is change, all is illusion."

Ma stood up and gathered her basket. "Thank you for the honey, Mistress Alice."

Anne had brought out four stone jars sealed with wax. Ma and Mistress Alice curtseyed to each other again.

"Thank you for the royal Wedding gift, Mistress Smith."

To the surprise of the children, the two women embraced warmly. They seemed to cling to each other for a moment.

"Come twins, come Lily and Emmet."

Ma began to walk swiftly out of the garden. Emmet, hurrying along by her side whilst waving awkwardly to Mistress Alice, noticed that Ma's eyes were bright. He slipped his hand tentatively in hers.

"Ma...?"

"It's alright Emmet," Ma spoke sharply and gave his hand a shake. "Change is coming, that's all. I can smell it on the wind."

There was no wind, and Emmet didn't understand what she meant. How could anyone smell change? It made no sense. None of the afternoons happenings had made sense, but he felt that asking Ma what it meant would be fruitless. He kept on holding Ma's hand, though. He loved his mother dearly and didn't like to see her sad, for whatever reason.

3. St. John's Eve

It was a quiet party that made their way back to Barley Village. Ma seemed deep in thought and the mead had made everyone sleepy. Lily, riding high on Emmet's shoulder, her precious egg slung in its bag over her arm and her grubby thumb plugged firmly into her mouth, kept falling asleep, then waking with tiny starts as she slid down Emmet's head. Emmet himself was hot and uncomfortable under his heavy burden but knew better than to complain. Even the twins were unusually silent.

As they walked the last lap, through the village to the Smithy, Pa was looking out for them and came to relieve Emmet of his load.

"Well done, son," he said with a grin. "She may not think she's big yet, but she's big enough when you have to carry her."

Emmet flexed his shoulders in relief and gratefully felt the cool breeze on his sweaty skin. Pa carried sleeping Lily into the cottage and laid her gently on a pile of sheepskins in the corner.

"Let her have her sleep out," he said, "or she'll not be able to stay awake for the fun."

All the villages had bonfires to celebrate St. John's Eve. Fires were lit up and down the country on the highest points to encourage it to shine brightly and ripen the crops. It was a time of feasting, jollity and, for the men at least, serious drinking of ale and mead. The twins loved it and seemed to have thrown off their earlier tiredness in the excitement of helping their mother pick flowers and herbs from the garden. They brought them to Pa and Emmet seated outside the forge who skilfully wove them into garlands for heads and necks. St. John's wort, vervain and mugwort were woven in with six other herbs. The twins didn't know all the names, but they knew them by sight, and that was the important thing. Ma, too, seemed her old self again, laughing with the twins as they gathered the flowers.

17

"More St. John's wort, Hetty," she said. "And Letty, lots more mugwort. It's such a good protection against illness. Today is the best day to pick it. I want lots to dry in the house."

The sun was still bright, but shadows were beginning to lengthen. A great pile of oaken branches had been carried up Pendle Hill by the men of the village earlier that day, and already people were beginning to make their way up with baskets of food and drink, everyone carrying an oak branch or stick. There was much singing and gaiety, the villagers wearing their garlands and posies, the children running and skipping.

"Time to wake Lily," Pa said. "Come on little maid."

He tried to wake her, shaking her gently in her nest of sheepskins.

"Nooo," whispered Lily, flushed and drugged with sleep, and pushed her thumb further into her mouth. The twins were less gentle.

"Lily, Lily," they shouted, "wake up. We'll go without you."

That roused her.

"Nooo," she wailed again. "Don't go without me. I'm not big."

Ma and Pa laughed at their daughter's indignation.

"Look Lily," said Emmet kindly. "I've made you a garland. Are you going to put it on?"

He helped her up on still wobbly legs and placed the garland on her untidy curls. Lily was enchanted.

"Take it off again, I want to look at it first."

Emmet obligingly lifted it off. Lily took it in her hands and admired it from every angle before finally burying her nose in it and sniffing ecstatically.

"It's perfect," she pronounced at last, and jammed it back on her head. "Come on everyone. I want to go."

They all laughed at that. Pa and Emmet picked up the laden baskets which Ma and the twins had prepared that morning and, with their sticks in their hands, the Smith family joined the procession of villagers, Hetty and Letty tearing up

18

and down like mad things.

"Calm down you two," said Ma. "You'll be worn out and fit for nothing before we even get there."

It was a beautiful evening, clear and bright and still. The villagers were dressed in their best clothes and there was a holiday feel of excitement and happiness, the air of a crowd determined to enjoy itself. Hetty and Letty joined a gaggle of other girls who skipped and sang their way up Pendle Hill.

The bonfire was built at the top. Villagers sat in family groups or with friends and neighbours on sheepskins and blankets, eating, drinking and chattering. Emmet could see the Demdike family – Old Demdike herself, her daughter Elizabeth and her grandchildren, Alison, who was almost grown up, Jimmy and Jennet. They sat quiet and self-contained, apart from the other groups. Jimmy, as usual, had Henny Penny with him, and she wandered about, pecking at imaginary worms. People greeted them with polite deference, but nobody sat with them. Emmet felt awkward. He felt he should speak to Jennet, or acknowledge her in some way, but felt shy about going over. He looked in her direction, but she steadfastly refused to meet his gaze, and after a while he gave it up.

Another family also was not in the main party. Old Chattox, another Cunning Woman, with her daughters Elizabeth and Anne, sat demurely on the outskirts. Ma dropped both groups a polite curtsey as she passed. Emmet realised that Anne was the woman who worked at Roughlee Hall, the one who had served them mead and gingerbread. There was only muted, polite acknowledgement. It seemed to Emmet that the villagers did not wish to anger the witches by ignoring them, but at the same time did not wish to appear too friendly. It was a difficult tightrope to walk, and no one appeared comfortable doing so.

A new figure made her way sedately up the hill. Mistress Alice. She greeted everyone she met with great courtesy, witches and villagers alike.

"A fine evening, Mistress Demdike, is it not? Mistress

Brown, I congratulate you on the birth of your new little one. Master James, I trust your rheumatism improves in this warm weather?"

Everyone bowed or bobbed curtsies to the Lady of the Manor, and as she drew near to the great pile of wood, Pa stepped forward respectfully.

"Mistress Alice, would you do us all the great honour of lighting the Midsummer Fire?"

He handed her a flaming torch. She thrust it into the dry straw at the centre of the pyre. Pa worked the bellows he'd carried up with him and soon the bonfire burst into flames. A hearty cheer went up from the watching villagers.

Looking away across the land, Emmet could see the smoke and flames of more fires. He felt a warmth and happiness somewhere in the centre of his being, imagining other villages enjoying their fires together. 'Maybe all over the world,' he thought to himself. It was a wonderful thought that warmed him as much as the fire itself.

By now the sun had sunk below the horizon and the evening star could be seen brilliant and shining in the fading blue haze of sky. The firelight flickered on the faces of the villagers as they danced and sang ancient songs from a time long forgotten, tripping strange measures which all seemed to know, yet none remembered being taught. The men drank deeply whilst the women's laughter had a note of reckless wildness in it. Emmet was whirled by the dancers. He forgot his spots, he forgot his awkwardness. He stamped and twirled and sang as lustily as the best of them. Time seemed to stand still.

Jennet's hand touched his. She looked up at him with her cool green gaze. "It's time," she whispered. "The moon is rising."

Emmet followed her pointing finger. Sure enough, the moon hung in the night sky just above the horizon, a beautiful round lamp, bright and low and bigger than Emmet had ever seen it.

"Come," she said, and gave his hand a tug. "Jimmy and

the girls are waiting."

Emmet, dazed by the fire and the wild dancing, allowed her to tow him out of the throng, into the shadows beyond the circle of firelight. Jimmy stood, a pixie-like figure, holding Lily by the hand, Henny Penny tucked under his other arm. The twins were next to him, their long, fair hair mad and dishevelled from the dancing.

"Come on, Emmet." Hetty was impatient. "What are you messing about at? You're always last. Don't you want your spots healed?"

Emmet could only nod, dumbly. He felt slightly dizzy and disorientated from all the whirling. Jennet let go of his hot hand and beckoned the group away from the firelight, away from the frenzied dancers and down the hillside in the direction of the Holy Well. Away from the fire, their skin cooled, and Emmet shivered. Distant voices of the villagers became a faint drone.

Jennet led them down to the Holy Well where they all sat on the damp moss in a circle. No one spoke. Lily's eyes were like saucers, and even Henny Penny stopped her usual contented chicken sounds. Jennet silently traced a circle around them, widdershins. She whispered a charm half under her breath, strange words running into each other that the children couldn't quite catch. She took a stone bottle, uncorked it, and bid Emmet cup his hands. She poured clear liquid into them and a wonderful smell wafted up, of roses, yes, but also familiar herbs and spices. Lily thought of the smell of their mother's arms when she held her close. Emmet knew it smelt of Jennet's hair, if he was only allowed to bury his face in it.

"Quickly, Emmet!" Jennet brought them to themselves. "Rub it over your face, where the spots are. Try not to spill any."

Emmet brought his hands up to his face. For a moment he thought the scent was so strong it would overpower him, but he did as he was told. At first it burnt, but the burning was more ice than fire. A cool, delicious sensation passed over his face and, after some moments, he knew that his skin was clear.

He took his hands away. Letty and Hetty gasped. Lily was the first to speak.

"Emmet, they've truly gone! I'd forgotten how nice your face is."

This was a somewhat backhanded compliment, but Emmet was delighted.

"Thank you, Jennet," he said quietly.

He couldn't think what else to say. He was delighted. This was the first charm Jennet had performed on her own, and the result was entirely satisfactory.

"Hold out your hands everyone," she commanded.

The girls all held out their hands and Jennet poured a little into each of their outstretched palms.

"Now rub your eyes," she said.

"Won't it sting?" Lily was worried.

"No," Jennet said reassuringly. "It has rue and fennel in it for clear sight."

The girls obediently rubbed their eyes.

"Although there wasn't anything wrong with them in the first place," muttered Letty.

"I said clear sight, not eyesight," answered Jennet, tartly. "There is much to see on St. John's Eve, if your sight is clear."

Jimmy, who had sat motionless all this time, like a comical figure carved out of stone, spoke.

"Time for special egg." He patted Lily's bag. "Special egg, Lily. Where your special egg? Time to use it."

Lily opened the linen bag. Carefully, with the rather stertorous breathing that accompanied any act of concentration, she eased the nest out of the bag and laid it on one of the stones. The moonlight shone down on it and Emmet could see that his impression earlier in the afternoon was not a trick of the light. The egg was glowing with rainbow colours, but under the full moon, with an astonishing intensity.

They gazed at it. The rainbow light grew brighter and a silvery beam shone across the night sky, connecting it to the moon. The children became aware of a humming sound, not loud but low and strong. Emmet could feel it deep inside

22

himself, somewhere at the pit of his stomach. At first, he thought confusedly that Jennet must be making the noise, but then he realised that it was coming from the egg itself. The sound became stronger and even the rocks around them seemed to vibrate. As the children began to fear that they couldn't bear it any longer, they became aware of a shape moving, flickering in the depths of the egg. The sound reached a crescendo and everyone put their hands over their ears. There came a resounding crack! The rainbow egg burst asunder and out from the pieces of the shell there emerged a tiny silver hare.

The silence that followed the hatching of the egg was so abrupt and complete after the tumultuous humming that it made Emmet's ears ring. The hare sat up on its hind legs and began to clean its ears. It was growing, slowly and gracefully, until it was slightly larger than an ordinary hare. It regarded the company steadily with eyes like the moon.

"A wish," it said, and Lily thought afterwards that its voice was like the singing of the stars, if stars could sing. "A wish each, for St. John's Eve."

With one bound it was on the beam of light, speeding up it, so it seemed, towards the moon. It called back over its shoulder, faintly in its star-song voice, "Be careful, so careful, what you wish for."

The beam of light, the speeding silver beast, faded in the night sky. They gazed and gazed until it had completely vanished and all that was left was the bright, unblinking moon.

"Emmet," breathed Hetty and Letty together, "what shall we wish for?"

Emmet didn't know. Two days ago, before he had met the witch's children, his heart's desire, he would have told anyone who asked, would have been for his spots to vanish. Now he was somewhat at a loss. Naturally thoughtful by nature, he couldn't summon up a new heart's desire at the drop of a hat. However, Lily was a different kettle of fish. She knew exactly what she wanted to wish for, and she didn't hesitate.

"I wish I was big!" she cried, in a loud, clear voice.

23

For a split second she remained small, chubby, happy Lily, bright and hopeful in the moonlight. Next, she gave a terrible, wrenching scream that pierced Emmet's heart and made his blood run cold. Everything around them seemed to waver and come apart at the seams, as though the stuff of the universe was re-arranging itself in some complicated pattern, just for a moment. The air became still. Emmet reached out for his sister, but she seemed to have vanished. In her place, two large tree trunks seemed to be growing, their roots like feet in front of them.

"Lily," Emmet felt icy panic grab his stomach, "where are you?"

"I'm here!" wailed Lily from high above his head.

The nearest tree root moved and knocked Emmet, Jimmy and the girls over so that they tumbled together in a heap of arms and legs. Henny Penny gave a frightened squawk and fluttered onto Jimmy's shoulder as everyone scrambled up. They gazed, horrified at what stood before them. The tree trunks were not tree trunks at all. They were Lily's legs. Lily had wished with all her heart to be big, and big she had become. She towered above their heads, a five-year-old giantess, sobbing hysterically. A great fat tear fell on Emmet's head. It was like a whole bucketful of water, lukewarm, and slightly salty.

"Don't cry, Lily," Emmet tried to calm the howling child. "Please don't cry. You're soaking us."

"I don't like being big," wept poor Lily. "I only wanted to be a bit big. I didn't want to be enormous big."

"Lily," called Jennet, "it's alright. One of us will wish you small again."

Lily peered down at them all from her lofty height.

"Can you?"

"Of course," said Jennet. "We've all got a wish each, remember. It just means one of us will have to not wish anything for themselves, that's all."

Everyone looked expectantly at each other. It was a difficult moment. They all wanted Lily to be her proper size

24

again, of course they did, but nobody wanted to give up their wish. The silence became uncomfortable. Hetty spoke at last.

"You should do it, Emmet," she said. "You're the oldest."

"Sometimes," began Emmet bitterly, "I wish I wasn't."

"Emmet," said Jennet with a warning in her voice, "be careful what you wish for."

But it was too late. The universe began to re-arrange itself again. Emmet's stomach did a back flip. The wavering, coming apart-at-the-seams feeling died down. Nothing seemed to have changed. Lily was still big, and Emmet, as far as anyone could see, was still the oldest.

"Well, go on then Emmet," Letty scolded. "Use your wish. Make Lily small again. You're supposed to take care of us," she added, sanctimoniously.

"He can't," said Jennet. "He already has. Used his wish, I mean."

"But nothing happened."

The twins were bewildered.

"Yes, it did." A voice behind them spoke. "Emmet isn't the oldest. He never was. I am."

Everyone turned to the speaker. Even Lily stopped crying in astonishment.

Another band of children stood in the moonlight beside the well. Three boys and two girls. Even in the moonlight which bleached everything of colour, they appeared deathly white, and they were dressed in tattered grave clothes. There came with them a strange, earthy smell. Letty and Hetty held tight to Emmet's hands.

"Who are they?" whispered Letty.

"Emmet knows us, don't you, Emmet?" said the smallest girl. "Do say you haven't forgotten us." She spoke reproachfully. "We've never forgotten you."

There were tears in Emmet's eyes. When he spoke, his voice wobbled.

"How could I forget you, Rosie. Janie, don't we always come and lay flowers on your grave? Charlie, you used to carry me on your shoulders, and Will and John, you used to

25

take me fishing in the stream."

Lily gave a delighted shriek, the blast of which almost knocked them all over.

"Make me small someone, please! I want to hug Rosie. And I don't want to squash her," she added.

Jimmy patted her huge foot. "Wish my Lily was her right size again," he said loudly, and his voice was clearer than they had ever heard it. The re-arrangement of the universe was smoother this time.

Lily, tear-stained and wildly dishevelled, stood in their midst, Lily-sized once more, and the best size of all to be, she thought. She flung herself on Jimmy and hugged him, planting a big wet kiss on his cheek.

"Thank you, kind Jimmy. I love you best in all the world." Lily was expansive. She turned to Rosie, uncertain now. "Can I hug you Rosie? Are you real or are you a ghost?" she asked, fearfully.

"I'm a real ghost," said Rosie, "but I'm still your sister."

She came up to Lily, put her wraith-like arms around the chubby body and her cold cheek against Lily's warm one. For a moment the ghost child and the living child embraced tenderly. It was like hugging moonbeams, Lily thought.

"We love your presents, Lily," said Janie. "Look, I'm wearing the stone with the hole in it."

The stone was hung around her ghostly neck on what seemed to be a length of horsehair.

"And I've got the magpie's feather," Rosie said. She had stuck it behind her ear at a jaunty angle.

"We can't eat the food you leave," said Will, "but we enjoy looking at it and smelling it, and then we feed it to the animals that live in the graveyard."

"What's it like, being dead?" Letty asked, a sensible enough question.

"It just is," replied Charlie. "You don't get bigger or older. Nothing can hurt you any more. We don't need to eat or drink."

"I miss that," John broke in, wistfully. "Sometimes, if I

try hard, I can almost remember what Ma's rabbit stew tasted like. Only almost though," he sighed.

Letty felt so sorry for him that she forgot to be frightened and squeezed his wasted hand. She loved Ma's rabbit stew. The thought of never tasting it again was too terrible to contemplate.

"It's alright though," Janie spoke comfortingly. "We've lots of company."

The idea of a whole village of dead people going about their business was disturbing. Perhaps dying wasn't the terrible thing everyone always seemed to think.

"Why can't people see you?" asked Hetty. "They might not be so sad if they knew you were alright."

"There are laws," Will said. "Life is life and death is death. They are like oil and water, they don't mix. They are as different as any two things can be. And there are mysteries, things we can't tell you even if we wanted to. The only thing that can sometimes mix the two is magic." He glanced at Jennet. "*She* knows that."

Jennet said nothing.

"Magic brought us here," Rosie sang. "You wished, Emmet, and here we are, but only until sunrise. The laws are different at Midsummer. If you had wished yesterday or the day after tomorrow, we would not be here, but you wished at the perfect time."

Her happiness was infectious. The children joined hands, dead and living together, a ragged circle, and began to dance, the steps as old and wild as the ones still being danced around the great bonfire on the other side of Pendle Hill. There was music, but where it came from, whether it was the music of the stars or the singing of their own hearts, they couldn't tell. Their feet were like floating feathers, like moths, lighter than air. When Jennet tried to remember afterwards, it seemed to her that perhaps they hadn't danced on the earth at all.

At last they grew weary, and one by one they collapsed, panting and giggling on the rough grass. They lay still, in a circle, heads close together in the centre, legs pointing outwards like the spokes of a wheel, gazing up into the night sky. The music had faded and for a moment all was silent, the stars of the Milky Way like a celestial highway arching to infinity above their heads.

Another sound was heard, distant and almost imperceptible at first, but closer and closer, the bell-like baying of hounds.

"A hunt," thought Emmet, "but who could be hunting at night? And what?"

The stars seemed to blink and waver as though something had passed across them. As the children gazed, awestruck, a pack of giant and ghostly hounds streamed across the night sky above their heads. Amongst them was what seemed for a moment like a giant stag, but then they saw that it was a mighty hunter on horseback with huge, magnificent antlers growing from his head. His long wild hair streamed out behind him with the wind of his going, a spear held in one massive hand, muscles bulging over armbands of intricately wrought gold. For a split second it seemed to the children that he saw them and his glittering eyes narrowed, dark and fierce in the hawk-like pride of his face. He raised his hunting horn to his lips and blew a long blast. As the notes died away, so did the hunt fade from sight, as though passing into another part of the heavens where their earthly eyes could not follow.

"Who was it?" Emmet asked, breathless.

"The Wild Hunt," said Charlie. "They always hunt at the Feast of St. John. Change is coming. It's in the wind."

Emmet stared. Someone else had said the same thing. Where? Who? Of course! His mother, that afternoon, on the way home from Roughlee Hall. Could it have only been that afternoon? He opened his mouth to ask a question, but Jimmy spoke first.

"See moon!"

The moon was hanging low on the horizon. The stars had faded and the sky was becoming lighter.

Jimmy spoke again. "Jennet, Hetty, Letty, make wishes. Almost sunrise."

28

The three girls stood in consternation. The night's events had been so exciting that they had completely forgotten about their wishes. Now, the moon was fading fast. One bird and then another began to sing.

"It's the dawn chorus." Charlie's voice was urgent. "Wish quickly, before it's too late."

His voice was faint, and the ghostly children were growing harder to see as the sky grew brighter.

Hetty and Letty looked into each other's eyes. They held each other's hands.

"I wish we could always understand the language of creatures," Letty spoke quickly.

"I wish we could always see the unseen things," Hetty spoke seamlessly behind her so that the universe only re-arranged itself once, but more violently, as though it resented having to grant two wishes at once.

"Come on Jennet," Emmet spoke anxiously. "Don't lose your wish."

Jennet gazed at him desperately, biting her lip. What to wish for? If only there was more time.

"I wish... I wish..."

The universe quickly turned itself inside out and back again. The sun broke over the horizon. It was Midsummer Day.

"What did you wish for?" Lily wanted to know.

Jennet blushed. "It was a private wish," she said quickly.

"That's not fair," Hetty and Letty said together, indignantly. "You heard everyone else's wishes."

"Leave her alone," Emmet was kind. "She can have a private wish if she wants, can't she, Charlie?" But when he turned to his brother, Charlie was nowhere to be seen. Charlie, Will, John, Janie and Rosie had faded away like morning mist. All that was left was the faint, dying graveyard smell, and even that was almost gone.

"Charlie, Rosie?" Emmet's voice held the shrill note of tears. "Please come back."

Jimmy slipped his stubby hand into Emmet's.

"No cry, Emmet," he said. "Gone home to graveyard. Time to sleep. Us too," he added.

Hetty and Letty put their arms around their big brother.

"We will see them again you know," Hetty was reassuring. "We wished, didn't we?"

"My special egg is all broken," said Lily, and yawned so widely that it almost split her chubby face in two.

"Lily," said Jennet, "it had to break, didn't it, or the silver hare couldn't have come out of it."

"I know that," said Lily, "but I did like it."

"Never mind Lily," said Emmet. "We could collect the pieces if you like, and you could keep them to remind you."

They turned to the stone where the egg had hatched. The linen bag lay limp and damp from the morning dew. The fragments of shell no longer glowed with rainbow colours but looked just like the pieces of an ordinary hen's egg. Emmet bent to gather them up and started back in astonishment.

Everyone gathered round. There among the fragments of shell, winking brightly in the early morning sunlight, lay a tiny, beautifully wrought silver hare. Legs outstretched, it looked as though it had been forged in mid-run, and in the tip of one of its long ears was a hole, so that it could be hung on a chain and worn around the neck.

Lily picked it up and held it reverently in her palm.

"Lily," breathed Hetty, a note of envy in her voice, "you are lucky."

The silver hare was undoubtedly Lily's, but there was a collective and wistful silence. Each child yearned to be the fortunate owner of this lovely thing. Lily looked at them all for a moment. Complicated emotions passed over her small face. She appeared to be wrestling with some inner conflict.

"We'll share it," she announced, generously, "but I get to wear it first," she insisted.

"Kind Lily."

Jimmy stroked her untidy curls. He picked up Henny Penny and tucked her under his arm.

The children were tired, hungry, and extremely cold. The

30

twins, skinniest of all the band, were shivering and their teeth were beginning to chatter.

"Time to come home."

A much loved and welcome voice spoke behind them. Pa stood there with Ma by his side. He slung a sheepskin around Emmet's shoulders. Ma carried rolled up woollen shawls tucked under her arm. She wrapped them around the shoulders of her shivering daughters.

"Fancy being out all night with next to nothing on. I've never seen the like! Do you want to catch your death of cold? As if I haven't enough children lying in the graveyard as it is."

Emmet and the twins exchanged glances. Whatever their older brothers and sisters did in the privacy of their own graveyard, they didn't think much time was spent lying down. Jennet and Jimmy stood apart, holding hands rather forlornly, looking as though they felt left out. Emmet opened his mouth to ask Pa if they could come home for breakfast with the Smith family, but another, rather formidable figure with a lopsided face and a clay pipe clamped between its teeth appeared behind Ma and Pa.

"Mistress Demdike, good morrow to you."

Ma swept a deep curtsey, as though the old, frayed figure was royalty. Pa bowed low and doffed his cap. Old Demdike nodded to them regally.

"Granny!"

Jennet's pretty face lit up and she flew to her grandmother's side. Jimmy waddled over, grinning happily. Old Demdike enfolded her grandchildren tenderly in her tattered cloak.

"Time to rest, time to eat, time to bide a while and we'll see you at the royal wedding."

She nodded at the Smiths again, and she and Jennet and Jimmy seemed to vanish before their eyes. Emmet blinked, but nothing appeared strange to him this morning.

"Rest and eat and bide a while, an excellent plan. Come, my love," and Pa offered Ma his arm. She curtsied and took it. He hoisted Lily over his other shoulder and Emmet and the

twins followed them up over the brow of the hill.
  It was going to be another perfect day.
  Another perfectly extraordinary day.

4. THE ROYAL WEDDING

Hetty and Letty woke as they always did at the same moment. The sun was shining brightly through the window of their tiny sleeping chamber, lighting up Lily's golden curls. She was still sound asleep, the silver hare clutched tightly in her chubby fist in the feather bed the three sisters shared. The twins looked at each other in silence, all the events of the previous night flooding through their minds.

"Did we?" Letty asked softly.

"We must have," said Hetty. "Look, Lily's got the silver hare. It truly happened."

The iron latch on the bedroom door lifted, the door opened and Ma poked her head inside.

"Good," she said, "you're awake. Get Lily up and come down for breakfast. We mustn't be late for the Royal Wedding."

She disappeared again, and the twins made faces at each other. Lily was notoriously hard to wake, and often grumpy if disturbed before she was ready. However, just as the girls were bracing themselves for the tussle which was sure to come, Lily gave such a loud and sudden snort in her sleep that she woke herself up and sat bolt upright in bed.

"My special egg!" she exclaimed loudly, then she too remembered the night's happenings and opened the hand which held the silver hare.

"Whose go is it next?" Letty was hopeful.

"Jimmy's," said Lily firmly, "because he saved me from being big." She shuddered at the memory. "And because he gave me the special egg in the first place."

Letty sighed. She knew that this was fair but hoped she wouldn't be last. Her gaze turned to the window.

"Hetty, Lily," she whispered, "look, but be quiet."

On the stone window sill, in a warm patch of sunlight, lying back with its tiny arms behind its head for all the world as if sunbathing, was a miniature person, about the size of a child's hand.

"It's a fairy," said Lily in wonder

Ever so quietly, the girls slid out of bed and tiptoed over to the window. They stood staring down at the tiny figure in amazement and delight.

"It was my wish," Hetty whispered. "I wished for us to be able to see the unseen things. I never thought of fairies."

The creature opened its eyes. For a moment it surveyed the children calmly, then a look of growing annoyance spread over its minute face.

"You can see me!" it cried in a silvery voice. "How can you? That's just plain wrong."

The fairy leapt to its tiny feet, spread delicate, moth-like wings and was out of the open casement in a flash, pausing only to give the girls a look of indignant fury before vanishing into the sunlit garden.

"Goodness," said Letty at last, "wasn't she angry?"

"It must have been a shock for her," said Hetty. "Perhaps that's her favourite spot and she's used to being there in private. We must have startled her."

Lily was worried. "I want to see the fairies, but I don't want to make them angry."

"It's alright, Lily," said Letty. "Let's get dressed and have breakfast. If we see any more fairies, we'll try to pretend we can't."

They wore their best gowns with clean aprons. As quick as they were, Emmet was ready before them, delighted that his skin was clear. He kept touching his face to remind himself of the miracle.

"You look fine, son," said his mother.

"Aye," said Pa, "young Jennet did a good job."

Breakfast was day old bread, eggs and honey, curds and whey, and all the children ate hungrily. Ma combed the girls' hair and braided it with ribbons. Pa and Emmet put on their Sunday hats, and once more the Smith family set off for Roughlee Hall.

Even though it was almost noon, the village was quiet.

Not a soul was to be seen abroad, despite the hot sunshine. All, it seemed, were lying abed, sleeping off the late night and excessive drinking of St John's Eve. Lily walked between Hetty and Letty, holding tight to their hands, the silver hare hanging around her neck on a long twist of yarn, gleaming in the sunlight. Every now and then she gazed around, half fearful of more enraged fairies. As they walked through the village they saw nothing out of the ordinary, but once they had crossed the bridge over Pendlewater, away from human habitation, small shapes flitted amongst the grass and curious faces peeped out from bushes and trees. One small and ugly goblin made a hideous grimace, crossing his eyes and sticking out his tongue at Lily who gave a small squeak of fright.

"What is the matter, Lily?" asked her mother.

"It's the fairies, Ma, they are making horrible faces at me."

Emmet expected Ma to tell Lily not to be so silly, but once again she surprised him.

"They won't hurt you, Lily. Fairies never hurt anyone, although sometimes the goblins can be rather mischievous. Make a face back, don't let them think you are frightened."

"Ma!" Hetty and Letty were astonished. "Can you see fairies too?"

Pa chuckled. "Your Ma is the seventh daughter of a seventh daughter. She sees all kinds of things."

Ma gave him a sharp look, tossed her head and sniffed.

"I see you, Master Smith," she remarked tartly, darting at the still grimacing goblin and fetching it a deft clip around one of its large, pointed ears. The goblin howled, stopped its gurning and glared at her reproachfully, rubbing the afflicted ear.

"If the wind changes, you'll stay like it," Ma told it sternly. "You're ugly enough as it is without making matters worse. Stop frightening Lily."

Ma took Pa's arm and continued, head held high. "Come along children, don't dawdle."

They were now approaching the stand of trees where

they'd seen the silvery brown hare that had taught Roger Nowell a lesson the day before. Nine hares now crouched in a large circle in the shade of the trees.

"Look Pa," said Emmet, pointing. "I've never seen so many hares together."

Pa glanced over casually and doffed his hat to the hares. "Wedding guests, no doubt. They'll be there ahead of us, that's certain."

As he spoke, as though at a given signal, the hares shot off like a volley of silvery brown arrows in the direction of Roughlee Hall. A skirl of swallows swooped over the grass behind them, snapping up flies as they went, and with their new-found sight the children could see that on the back of each one rode a tiny sprite. High above their heads, a skylark sang. The world, Emmet thought, was brimming over with magic. The ground beneath their feet hummed with it. He felt an excitement so strong that it was in danger of fizzing out, like the sparks from his Pa's anvil.

Roughlee Hall hove into view and Emmet saw the delicate figure of Jennet, sunlight burnishing her wild red hair, standing with Anne Chattox amongst the flowers. She waved when she saw the Smiths, and as they came through the garden gate he could see that she wore a garland of pink and yellow roses, making a wonderful contrast to her flaming tresses. Jennet and Anne held baskets, Anne's containing small posies and Jennet's wreaths of flowers. The girls bobbed curtsies and Jennet presented Ma and the girls with a wreath each for their hair, Anne pinning posies onto Pa and Emmet's jerkins.

"Come on round," said Jennet. "You're the last guests to arrive. It's almost time."

Anne led the way through the sunny garden, around the side of the building, lying quiet in the midday sun. As they came out to the back of the hall, the children gasped in wonder and delight. More tables had been set end to end and covered with spotless white linen cloths so bright in the intense light it almost hurt the eye to look at them. They were laid with pewter tankards and platters, and stone jars of roses were dotted here and there. All the straw beehives were bedecked with garlands of flowers.

"It's like fairyland," whispered Lily.

Mistress Alice stepped forward to greet them. She was richly dressed in embroidered silks and velvets, more like the well-to-do gentlewoman she truly was than the countrywoman she usually appeared.

"Mistress Alice," Lily beamed, "you look beautiful, just like a queen."

"Thank you, Lily. I bid you all welcome on this most auspicious day. Master Smith, Mistress." She curtsied deeply to them all. Pa and Emmet doffed their hats and bowed low whilst Ma and the girls swept curtsies in return.

"Do please come and join our other guests."

They followed her obediently further into the garden. The children could see, to their wonder and delight, that it was indeed like fairyland. The fairy-folk thronged the garden and to Lily's great relief none of them seemed angry. There were tall and slender elves with serious faces and eyes as green as grass, rather like Jennet's, he thought. There were beautiful fairies, flower-like in their myriad colours and shapes, wings like moths and butterflies, half-transparent, shimmering in and out of focus like the stuff of dreams. There were many of the small, ugly goblins telling each other risqué jokes, digging each other in the ribs, laughing raucously. There were bearded gnomes with pointed ears and short legs, shining daggers in their belts, keen dark eyes flickering constantly over the throng. It occurred to Emmet with a slight shock that they were guards.

In amongst the fairy people stood the Chattox and Demdike families, resplendent in their best clothes. With Jimmy was a taller and slightly older girl of about seventeen or eighteen. She was plumper and plainer than Jennet but had the same flaming red hair and green eyes.

"My sister Alison," said Jennet. Alison bobbed a curtsey and delightful dimples chased each other across her face. Normally, Emmet tried to hide from girls, plain or pretty,

37

because of the embarrassment of his spots. He had forgotten how it felt not to be self-conscious.

Jimmy held Henny Penny under his arm as usual, and today she wore a twisted garland of tiny flowers around her feathered neck - white violets, speedwell and lily of the valley.

"Henny Penny," Lily was enchanted, "you look so pretty."

"Thank you, Lily," said Henny Penny in a croaky, clucky kind of voice. Lily stepped back in astonishment, tripped over the large foot of a goblin close behind her and fell on her bottom with a bump. The goblin helped her up and dusted her down.

"A thousand pardons," he murmured with surprising politeness. "I trust your ladyship is not injured in any way?"

"I'm fine, thank you," Lily barely noticed him. "Henny Penny, you can talk!"

"Of course," Henny Penny croaked in amusement. "You couldn't understand me before, but thanks to your sister's thoughtful wish, you can. They are clever girls those sisters of yours. Give a child a wish and usually they waste it. Not those two. You can tell they are their mother's daughters."

"Henny Penny," said Emmet, "why did that goblin call Lily 'your ladyship'?"

"Because she is the daughter of one of The Five Families of course," said Henny Penny.

Emmet didn't understand and opened his mouth to say so, but before he had a chance to speak a large and important looking gnome, dressed in a splendid uniform, blew a fanfare on a golden trumpet. Instantly, the general hubbub and chatter died down.

"Let The Five be assembled. It is time."

The gnome's voice was dark and rich like plum cake, sounding as though it should have come from a much larger personage. The guests began to form a horseshoe shape around the beehives, and the children noticed for the first time that behind the hives, arranged facing them in a half-moon, were five wooden chairs, like thrones, most beautifully and intricately carved, with birds and beasts, suns, moons and stars. On the backs, in the centre of each, a hare, its ears sticking straight upwards.

One of the central hives was larger than the rest. Draped over it, weighted down by the garlands of roses, was Ma's beautiful piece of lace.

"Who will sit in the thrones?" whispered Lily who had slipped in between them.

The Queen, who had been hovering over the hive for a moment, alighted as she had done before, fitting perfectly over the lace image of herself. The uniformed gnome stepped up to the hive and blew another fanfare.

"Make way, make way for The Five."

The throng of guests parted like a wave receding from the shore.

"The Five, The Five, make way for The Five," rippled through the crowd in excited whispers.

The children craned their necks to see better. To their astonishment, Old Demdike, Mistress Chattox, Alice Nutter, and... surely not... Ma ... wove their way through the parting throng, seating themselves on the wooden thrones. One throne remained vacant until a tall old woman with hawk-like features and golden hoops in her ears detached herself from the shadow of a large oak tree, glided across the garden and sat herself elegantly in it. Henny Penny chuckled softly.

"Aunt Salome Boswell," she whispered to the children. "She always likes to make an entrance. Gypsies are so dramatic."

There was silence for a brief moment, The Five sitting motionless, almost as though they were part of the carvings. The wooden hares' ears, now that the women were seated, looked as though they were growing out of their heads.

The sun had reached its highest point in the sky, everything in the garden shimmering with a golden heat haze. All the assembled party gazed expectantly towards the central hive and the heat haze seemed to shimmer and waver faster like the flickering of flames.

A familiar humming filled the air. As it grew stronger and louder, the flickering heat haze was forming itself into a shape growing more solid and more defined with every passing moment. The humming reached a tumultuous crescendo then died away. Standing before them, glowing with light, was the Silver Hare.

"Welcome," it said in its starry voice. "Welcome to The Five and their families," and it inclined its shining head to the throned women who returned the gesture with grave reverence.

"Welcome to the Faery Clans."

There was a rustling of silken skirts and wings and a doffing of hats as much bowing and curtseying took place.

"Welcome to the Egyptians."

Out from under the same tree that had concealed Aunt Salome Boswell, there materialised a group of strangers, men, women and children, all with dark eyes and black curls, exotically dressed and all with the same golden rings in their ears. The women did not curtsey, but the tribe bowed with great reverence to the Silver Hare and, slightly mockingly Emmet thought, to the assembled company.

"And welcome to Wayland Smith."

The children looked towards the person the hare was addressing and gasped in astonishment. It was Pa, but what a change seemed to have come over him! Always a big man, he seemed taller and broader than ever. On his head he wore a winged helmet and over his chest a curiously wrought breastplate. His great black beard streamed over it, and by his side hung a magnificent sword. He raised his clenched fist to his shoulder in an unmistakable gesture of fealty.

"That's not Pa, is it?" whispered Lily.

"I thought his name was William," said Emmet, stupidly.

"Renowned and celebrated Blacksmith to the Gods," Henny Penny explained patiently. "Thousands of years' experience. All the best Dwarfish smiths have served under him. There's never been a smith to equal him. We almost lost him a few centuries ago at the court of King Nidud, but he got

40

out of that one in the nick of ..."

She trailed off as the gnome with the trumpet fixed her with a steely eye. Emmet and his sisters exchanged incredulous looks. They felt as though their small, humdrum world of cottage, smithy and village had been rent asunder, exchanged for a weird and wonderful universe in which anything could happen and probably would. Emmet wondered whether they had ever truly known their parents at all. He had no time to ponder the matter further, though, for the Silver Hare was speaking again.

"Dear friends," it said, and there was a ripple of joy in its voice, "we have gathered here today in the home of our sister Mistress Alice to celebrate a most solemn and happy occasion. Let us all be upstanding for the Queen."

The Five rose to their feet. Most of the assembled throng were standing already, and everyone gazed at the bee, a bright smudge of black and orange, tiny wings a-glitter on the whiteness of the beautiful lace. Unearthly music began to play, wild and joyous, yet solemn at the same time, from a band of fairy musicians grouped together in the shade of an apple tree, their instruments the like of which the children had never seen. Hetty and Letty found themselves swaying in time to the rhythm. When the song died away, the Silver Hare spoke again.

"Let the Wedding Flight commence."

There was a ferocious buzzing. The Queen flew into the air and out of the hive followed nineteen bees.

"The Queen's suitors," whispered Henny Penny to Emmet. "They must catch her and mate with her on the wing. Then they will die and fall to earth."

"Poor suitors!" exclaimed Lily.

"It is a great honour for them, Lily," said Henny Penny, gently. "They are drone bees, and this is the reason they are alive, for this one moment of glory. They would not trade a hundred years of life for their short season of love."

Lily was uncertain about this exchange. "Well, I'm glad I'm not a bee."

41

Every eye was on the Queen. Higher and higher she flew, into the brightness of the sun, the drones zooming after her. Every now and then one would catch up with her. They clung together for a moment and then the tiny body of the drone would fall away to earth as the Queen continued her wild flight. At last only one drone was left. He and the Queen flew ever higher until they were tiny dots, almost too far up for the eye to see.

Emmet, shading his eyes with his hand finally saw, or thought he saw, the tiny dots merge into one. For a few seconds they hung there, in the eye of the sun, then the tiny body of the last valiant suitor began slowly spinning down to earth. A sigh, wistful but satisfied, arose from the watchers on the ground. The Queen made her descent and alighted once more on the white lace.

Mistress Alice arose from her throne and approached the Queen who hovered from the lace onto her outstretched hand. She bent her head to the bee, listening intently, then straightened up and addressed the congregation.

"Beloved friends, Her Majesty wishes me to convey her most heartfelt thanks to you all for witnessing the Royal Wedding. Now she is tired and must return to the hive to rest and be fed before she embarks upon her life's work. She wishes to bestow upon you all great blessings and bids you enjoy the feast which is prepared in her honour. Thank you, one and all."

The Queen buzzed once more then flew into the hive. She looked exhausted, and her tiny wings seemed bedraggled.

The important gnome blew his trumpet once more.

"Let the feasting begin!"

For a moment, all was confusion - fairies, elves, humans scurrying in every direction while the Smith children remained helplessly where they were, not knowing what was expected of them. Jennet ran up to them with a basket of fruit in her arms.

"Emmet, set this on the table and find a seat for yourself and Lily. Hetty and Letty, come and help me in the kitchens."

Emmet did as he was told and found seats for them both halfway down the table. The twins went with Jennet to the great stone flagged kitchen and found Anne Chattox directing elves and fairies with the food.

"Here Jennet, take this dish of marchpane. Hetty, carry the apple pie. Steady. Have you got it? Letty, you take the strawberries... no, not the cream as well, come back for that, you'll drop it if you try to carry too much in one go. Careful!"

This last was to a small gnome staggering under the weight of a flagon of mead almost twice his own size. Anne and a tall elf snatched it out of his arms just in time to avoid a catastrophe as the gnome toppled over in a heap. He remained where he fell and a huge snore shook his portly frame.

"Drunk," exclaimed Anne in annoyance. "I knew I should have locked the cellar. There's always one."

The tall elf grinned and shrugged his shoulders. He seized the inebriated one by his large ears, dragging him under the kitchen table, out of the way of all the helpers.

"Let him sleep it off," he said cheerfully. "He'll miss the feasting, that's punishment enough for sure."

Emmet and Lily sat watching round-eyed as the wondrous feast was piling up on the tables before them. Lily's thumb was plugged firmly into her mouth and she leaned against Emmet's shoulder, silently watching the hubbub around them.

There was pigeon pie, dishes of sallet fragrant with herbs, nettle cheese, rye bread and oat cakes, pats of yellow butter, bowls of junket, great jugs of thick cream and bowls piled high with strawberries and raspberries. There was quince conserve and dishes of green ginger and many kinds of sweetmeats that Emmet didn't recognise. Fairy food, perhaps. All the time the servers were rushing in and out with platters and jugs, the fairy musicians played a lilting fun-filled melody, fast and furious, parodying the frantic scurrying of the helpers.

All was in readiness. The Silver Hare was seated at the head of the table on a large throne like the others but carved only with a single eye. Mistress Alice, Pa and Ma sat on its right-hand side, and old Demdike, Mistress Chattox and Aunt

Salome Boswell on its left. The elves, fairies, gnomes and
goblins were crowded on benches, interspersed by the tribe of
Egyptians, the Chattox and Demdike clans and the children.
Some of the tinier fairies sat daintily on the table itself. When
everyone had a place, the Silver Hare drummed on its throne
with one of its powerful hind legs. A hush came over the
assembly.

"Dear Friends," it began, "a Blessing on this magnificent
feast."

Everyone linked hands, all the way around the table.

"Blessings on the feast," they chorused enthusiastically.
"Blessings on the cooks, blessed be!"

Pa raised his goblet which was brimming with mead.

"To the Queen, may the Great Mother bless her, and to
the suitors, may the earth receive them."

Everyone raised their goblets.

"To the Queen, to the suitors, blessed be."

"Now let the feasting begin."

The company needed no second bidding. There was much
hubbub as plates were passed and goblets filled, but it hushed
to a comfortable murmur as everyone began to eat. Emmet, his
plate full and his mouth fuller, thought he had never seen or
tasted more magnificent fare in his whole life. Jennet, seated
opposite him, caught his eye and gave him a look that touched
his heart. He couldn't ever remember having been so content.
Lily, munching her way through a huge dish of strawberries
and cream, heard a voice at her elbow.

"Would you pass me a piece of green ginger, please?"

Lily choked on a piece of strawberry. It was the fairy from
her bedroom windowsill who had been so furiously angry that
morning. Emmet thumped her absent-mindedly on the back
and she meekly passed the ginger.

"I'm so sorry we startled you this morning," Lily spoke
humbly. "We didn't want to upset you. It's just that you were
the first fairy we ever saw."

The fairy beamed at her.

"That's alright," she said cheerfully. "It was a shock,

44

that's all. I always have a nap there in the morning when it's sunny. Most children can't see me, so I was rather caught on the hop. I'm used to the idea now. Besides, your family are important to the Clans so I knew you would come into your power one day. Don't give it another thought. Shall we be friends? My name is Saffron."

Lily felt the knot of worry in her tummy dissolve and a warm feeling of relief engulf her.

"I'd love to be your friend. And I do think you are extremely pretty," she added.

The fairy simpered delightedly. "Thank you, Lily, I think you are, too."

Basking in the warmth of mutual admiration, they continued eating in companionable silence.

How long the feast lasted, Emmet couldn't tell. Well into the late afternoon, judging by the movement of the sun. Much was eaten, despite many of the guests being so tiny. Most of the platters and dishes were completely empty, some scraped so clean that any washing up would be superfluous.

The important gnome climbed up on his seat and blew on his trumpet again.

"It is time for the entertainment," he announced, in his rich, plum cake voice. "If the friends would like to follow me."

There was much shaking out of skirts and brushing-off of crumbs. Belts which had been loosened were hastily done up again, in some cases, with great difficulty. The Egyptians had disappeared from the company. Even Aunt Salome Boswell was no longer on her throne. Emmet wondered how they had vanished so unobtrusively. The fairy musicians began to play again, this time a mysterious tune filled with the promise of adventures about to happen.

The company followed the important gnome who seemed more important than ever and enjoying it profoundly. He led them beneath the tall oak tree into an orchard beyond. Ash poles and willow branches had been bent over and tied together to make frames, similar in shape to the beehives but much bigger, almost the size of shepherds' huts. Over the frames were laid large canvases to make cosy looking tents. The canvases were draped back to leave the entrances open against the heat of the day, and inside they were lined with exotic-looking carpets and sheepskins, and hung with gaily coloured silks, some embroidered with beads and sequins and tiny mirrors.

Lily was enchanted. "Oooh," she said breathlessly, "I wish we could live in one of those."

Behind the camp, for that was what it was, several horses and donkeys placidly cropped the grass. In the centre of the orchard there was a huge, ancient apple tree. Beneath it had been set up another decorated tent, somewhat larger than the others. Curtains were hung over the entrance concealing the interior, but in front of it was laid a particularly beautiful carpet. Next to it, Egyptian musicians, ready with their instruments, took up the fairy tune.

Some of the taller elves had carried out the thrones from the garden, and The Five, Wayland Smith and the Silver Hare were seated on them in front. The rest of the throng sat themselves on rugs and sheepskins, all murmuring excitedly to each other and gazing expectantly at the closed curtain. Emmet found himself seated next to Jimmy and Henny Penny with Jennet and his sisters around him.

"Henny Penny," he asked, "who are the Egyptians?"

The large hen shook her feathers in what must surely have been a shrug.

"They are a tribe, they travel all over the world. Who knows where they come from or where they go? Some people say they are descended from the survivors of the lost city of Atlantis. Some call them Bohemians, some Romanies. They themselves say they come from a place called Little Egypt so they call themselves Egyptians or Gypsies. What is certain is that they are a powerful, magical race knowing many mysteries. Aunt Salome Boswell is the Chovihani of this troupe and her powers are legendary."

"What is a Chovihani?" Emmet was intrigued.

"It is the Gypsy name for a Cunning Woman," said Henny

Penny. "Like all The Five, she has many magical powers. She can cast spells, shape shift and foretell the future. Indeed, she is perhaps the most powerful of them all. It does not do to cross her. The Chovihanis are a law unto themselves. Ordinary people would call her a witch, but that is a name that we do not use here."

Emmet opened his mouth to ask another question, but Jennet dug him in the ribs.

"Shh," she whispered, "it's starting."

The music died away and the curtain was drawn back by unseen hands. Everyone gasped. Exquisitely carved and dressed figures were revealed, a prince, a princess and others. There was a painted backcloth behind them of a beautiful palace and to Lily's astonishment the figures began to move. She clung to Emmet, fearful.

"What are they? Is it magic?"

Henny Penny gave a throaty chuckle. "They are puppets Lily. This is a puppet theatre. They are carved dolls. If you look hard, you can see they have strings attached to them. Some of the Egyptians are hidden behind the scenery, moving the strings. It's clever, nothing to be frightened of. Watch and listen. They are going to act out a story. It's called a play."

Reassured, Lily clamoured on to Emmet's knee, plugged her thumb into her mouth and settled down to watch. All the children were utterly spellbound. Living as they did in their tiny hamlet, far away from any town or city, they had never seen such a thing in their lives. It was beyond anything they could ever have imagined. They were used to the mumming, plays acted in the village on May Day and at Christmas, but that was just local people dressed up, nothing compared to this wondrous show. Even though no magic was used, it was magical.

The fairy clans loved it too and were vocal in their appreciation, singing along with all the music, cheering the hero and heroine and hissing loudly at the villain.

It was a long and complex tale, the Prince and Princess separated by the villain, having to endure many trials and

47

tribulations and harrowing adventures amid skilful scene changes, before the villain was conveniently dispatched by a magnificently carved lion sporting a mane of curled horsehair, when they were finally reunited to rapturous applause from the ecstatic audience.

The curtain went down for the last time and with it, the sun. The children, waking from the spell of the play as though from a dream, realised that lanterns had been lit all over the orchard, hanging from trees and inside the tents, reflecting tiny mirrors, and softening the velvety darkness. Someone had made a fire, and many of the throng sat around it. The musicians struck up again and one of the Egyptian women began to dance.

Like a carpet for royalty, the day rolled out wonder after wonder. Surely, there could be no more surprises after this?

5. WHAT AUNT SALOME BOSWELL SAW

The children stood together in a group, watching dreamily, when the important looking gnome approached them.

"Come with me," he said, in a soft voice. "You are wanted in the house."

He led them out of the orchard, past the beehives, shadowy and mysterious in the darkness, through the fragrant herb garden and into the great kitchen, lit by a single candle casting fantastic shadows on the stone walls and low-beamed ceiling. They passed through into a dining chamber with a huge round oak table in the centre, black and shiny with age and beeswax polish. Despite the warmth of the night, logs burned in the great stone fireplace and there was a smell like incense. Around the table were seated The Five, the Silver Hare, a tall elf, a fairy, and a goblin. The Hare spoke first.

"Welcome, Children of The Five. Be seated with us. You also Figwort. Welcome."

The assembled company looked serious, and Emmet, lifting small Lily onto a chair and seating himself, felt a tremor of anxiety until Pa caught his eye and gave him the ghost of a wink.

The Silver Hare gazed around at the gathering in silence for a moment, with its luminous, moon-like eyes. It bowed its head as though in sorrow, and Emmet felt a corresponding sadness in his own heart, although he could not have said why. It spoke gravely.

"Dear friends, in the midst of gaiety and joyful celebration, there comes also trouble. There is change in the wind. The wheel turns and so must we, to embrace that which comes, be it good or ill."

It turned its silvery head towards the children.

"Children of The Five, it is time for you to know your true heritage. The wisdom and the power of the Great Mother flows through your veins, and though you be mortal, you are not as other children."

Hetty and Letty looked at Emmet who felt he ought to say something.

"Please," he said, with some difficulty, "I... we... don't understand."

The Hare looked at him kindly.

"All of us here are bound to the Old Ways." Its gaze swept the room. "The ways of magic, of healing, the power in nature. But we live in dangerous times. There is a word for people who have such power, particularly if they are women. That word is 'witch'. It is a word we rarely use ourselves."

"These are the burning times. Across the English Channel our sisters are being burned in their thousands. Here, so far, they only hang us."

Pa made a sound, halfway between a snort and a sob. He wiped his mouth with the back of his hand.

"You wish to speak, Wayland Smith?" the Hare said gently.

"In the village," said Pa, "the word is whispered. Not about my wife, or myself, not yet. We have been careful. Mistress Alice also is above suspicion, so far. But Mistress Demdike and Mistress Chattox are viewed askance. A small flame has been lighted – how, or why, I do not know. But I tell you this. If a cow sickens or dies, if a child stops thriving or if a man is taken ill, the whispers grow louder, the flame is fanned and burns fiercer. The fingers of blame are pointed. It is easy for people to forget when they have been helped and healed. Easier still for them to believe they have been cursed."

There was a short silence. Mistress Alice moved uneasily in her chair.

"There is something else." She spoke slowly. "For many years now, my home has been open to all our kind, to the Egyptians and to the fairy clans. It has been a safe haven for us all, where we can perform our sacred rites and celebrate the seasons and grow our healing herbs in safety and security. Now this security is threatened. Roger Nowell, the magistrate is a hard and cruel man who casts his eyes towards my land. Many times has he visited me, often to cajole, in more recent months to threaten. He is determined to have it for himself. If for any reason I was – let us say – out of the way, his path would be clear."

Aunt Salome Boswell leaned forward. Her voice was deep and low, almost like a man's, and her speech was heavily accented.

"You wish that I should scry for you?"

The Silver Hare inclined his head.

"The time is right, my sister. To be forewarned is to be forearmed. Do that which is needful."

The firelight flickered on the gold hoops in Aunt Salome's ears.

"Wayland, may I use your breastplate?"

Pa silently unstrapped the beautifully wrought plate from his chest and set it wrong side up on the polished table so that it looked like a shallow bowl. Aunt Salome nodded in satisfaction.

"Mistress Alice, you have water from the Holy Well?"

"Of course."

Mistress Alice fetched a stone pitcher and poured some of the contents into it.

"Henny Penny, a feather, if you please."

Henny Penny hopped onto the table, twisted her head around and pulled out one of her own tail feathers, offering it to the old Egyptian with her beak. Aunt Salome took two candles and set one on either side of the scrying bowl.

"First," she said, "we must cast a circle. Figwort, do you set guards at the door?"

"It is done already, my lady," said Figwort, with just a touch of his habitual importance.

Aunt Salome began to pace a circle widdershins around the table. Next, she bowed in all the four directions: North, South, East and West. She took bread and salt from a dish, and crumbling the two together, passed around the dish with a goblet of mead. Everyone had a taste and a sip. Hands were clasped around the table for a moment, and then Aunt Salome Boswell sat herself down in front of the bowl. She took Henny

Penny's feather and stroked the surface of the water. The silence was profound and the children scarcely dared to breathe.

It seemed to Emmet that a silvery mist came up from the bowl as Aunt Salome peered into it intently. Minutes passed. At last the old woman snapped her fingers and seemed to shake herself.

"It is done."

She spoke bleakly.

"Well?" asked the Silver Hare. "Tell us what you see."

Aunt Salome regarded the company for a moment. Her face looked haggard in the candlelight and she seemed to have aged ten years. When she spoke, her voice was steady.

"It is bad," she said heavily, "as bad as it can be."

"Tell us!" Pa spoke hoarsely.

"We will not celebrate another Midsummer here together. Before Beltane next, my lady Demdike and my lady Chattox, and all their kin will be denounced as witches."

Old Demdike let out a cry of anguish.

"Even the little ones? Not my Jennet! My Scarlet Flower! Not my Jimmy!"

"All," repeated Aunt Salome. "And there is worse. Mistress Alice will be denounced too, and after Lammas tide..."

She faltered, but regained her composure, a pulse in her temple twitching.

"After Lammas tide you will all be hanged on Gallows' Hill."

There was a dreadful silence eventually broken by Lily bursting into loud and distraught sobs. Emmet thought that she was doing outwardly what everyone else was doing inside. For a few moments Lily was permitted to howl unchecked. Then Jimmy got up from his seat and put his stubby arms around her.

"No cry, Lily," he said, stroking her tangled curls. "Not over yet!"

"Jimmy is right." The Silver Hare spoke gravely. "Aunt

Salome has seen what will be if it is allowed to be. Life and death may take many courses. It is not often that we change the course with magic, but this time, we have a case for it."

Ma spoke for the first time. Her voice was bitter and shook.

"Seven years ago, when we had the diphtheria epidemic, we did not change this course with magic, and five of my children lie cold in the churchyard."

"Dear Heart," the Silver Hare spoke in a voice of great compassion, "you used all the powers of healing you had at your disposal, but their time had come. The Great Mother gives, and sometimes she takes. That is the law of Nature."

"Is it the law of Nature to lay violent hands on our sisters, on our brother, to put ropes around their necks and hang them for the crime of having wisdom that others do not possess?"

Ma bowed her head. She did not answer, but a single tear trickled down her cheek. Emmet did not dare look at Jennet. He thought back to the moment at the feast, sitting beside her, enjoying the puppet theatre. He remembered that he had only known her for two days but how she had already changed his life completely. A horrible image of Jennet hanging by her slender neck came unbidden into his mind, but at the same time the words of the Silver Hare gave him hope.

Pa held Ma's hand and put his other arm around her. He gave her a squeeze, kissing the top of her head, then spoke with authority.

"Because I have been favoured by the gods, although a mortal, I have lived many lifetimes beyond my allotted span. I have loved and lost because of this, not once, but many times. I have had my liberty taken cruelly from me, been condemned to a life in death at the court of King Nidud centuries ago, escaping solely by use of my wits. I say we save our sisters and our brother by whatever means we have at our disposal. Who will guard the Old Ways if we are lost?"

To Emmet, this seemed needlessly complicated, and his confusion must have shown because the Silver Hare said, "Speak, brother. All are free to speak here. What troubles you?

Tell us what is on your mind."

Emmet felt himself burning fiery red at being asked for his opinion.

"Please," he said nervously, "I don't know anything, and I expect I'm just stupid, but why can't Jennet and her family and the Chattox's and Mistress Alice just go away? Pack up their things right now and live somewhere else, before what Aunt Salome saw comes to pass?"

"That is an intelligent question," said the Silver Hare, approvingly, "and what you have suggested would seem to be, on the face of it, a sensible solution. However, we do not know the sequence of events leading up to the horror seen in the scrying bowl. If we attempt to change things before we see the full picture, we may find that we are part of these events, albeit unwittingly. We must allow events to unfold. Magic, like knowledge can be a dangerous thing. Used too lightly or at the wrong time can cause great harm."

He turned to old Demdike and old Chattox. Both looked uncomfortable.

"Sometimes a lack of care," it said pointedly, "can have grave and far-reaching consequences. I suspect that some of our number have not been as careful as they might have been."

Old Chattox became interested in an old portrait on the wall and old Demdike made a great show of filling her clay pipe with tobacco. The Hare gave a sigh.

"No matter, what is done is done."

The four representatives of the fairy clans had remained silent so far. Now they exchanged glances and the tall elf began to speak.

"Atterlothe at your service."

He was the same elf, Emmet noticed, who had helped Anne earlier with the drunken gnome. He was serious now, but smiled with sudden warmth at Emmet, catching his eye as he gazed around at the solemn gathering.

"The fairy clans support whatever course the Company of the Silver Hare decides to take. We do not scry as the Chovihani does, but we have watched the stars with interest for some time now, and the Wild Hunt is on the move. We propose that we all go away from here, the Cunning Women to their families, Aunt Salome Boswell to the Egyptians, we to the rest of our clans, consult with them and meet again at Lammastide. As the corn ripens, so I believe shall our way become clear. For now, it wants two hours until midnight. It is still Midsummer's Day, the last, Aunt Salome tells us, we shall spend together in this way, in this place. In the orchard sweet music plays, and there is dancing. There are still three turns of the seasons to enjoy before trouble meets us. To waste them is to insult the Great Mother. Come!"

6. An Unusual Family

The rest of the evening passed in a kaleidoscope of firelight, music and dancing. When Emmet tried to remember it, it seemed to him a blur. Nor could he remember the Smith family returning home, but they must have done, for he woke with a start the next morning to the sound of rain drumming on the window of the loft above the forge, which was his bedroom.

There was a feeling of dread in the pit of his stomach, which for a moment he could not put a name to, amongst the many extraordinary happenings of the night before. Aunt Salome Boswell's face filled his mind however and he remembered the terrible events her scrying had foreseen. Emmet felt sick at the memory. He lay completely still for a few minutes and then got up from his straw pallet, put on his boots and climbed down the loft ladder.

Pa was in the forge wearing his leather apron, busy lighting a fire in the bread oven. Without the winged helmet and the silver breastplate, there seemed nothing untoward about him; he just looked like Emmet's Pa, the village blacksmith, an ordinary man with an ordinary life. Emmet's head spun. It was all too much.

"Pa," he said.

"Now then lad, you've had a good sleep."

He gave Emmet a searching look, rose to his feet and enveloped his son in a great bear hug.

"Nay lad, don't take on, it's alright, it's all alright, you'll see. There lad, there."

Emmet had burst into tears, great silent wrenching sobs that hurt his chest. He wept for Jennet, for Jimmy, for Mistress Alice, but also for all the changes, both wonderful and terrible, that had happened to his life in the past two days. He knew that nothing would ever be the same again. He felt lost and out of his depth.

Pa, understanding something of this, simply held his son and let him cry. Emmet drew a deep breath.

"Handkerchief?" he asked in a waterlogged voice.

Pa pulled a rag from his pocket which might or might not at sometime have been a handkerchief and offered it to Emmet who blew his nose loudly.

"I'm alright now," he said shakily. "It was just, everything, you know?"

Pa patted his shoulder.

"Come on son, let's go and find the womenfolk. It's time Ma and I talked to you all."

They ducked through the small latched door that connected the forge to the cottage. Ma was kneading bread dough on the table. At the same moment the door which led to the staircase opened and in came the twins and Lily. All three looked white and pinched. Emmet could tell that they felt just as he did. Ma and Pa exchanged a quick glance.

"Sit you all down, children," Ma said. "I'm going to get you some bread and honey and some warm spiced milk. We are going to talk. Lily, is Saffron upstairs on the windowsill?"

"Yes, Ma."

Lily nodded, wan faced.

"Good," Ma was brisk. "Ask her to come down here a moment, would you please? There's a good girl."

Lily stumped back up the wooden staircase and returned with Saffron perched on her shoulder, grinning cheerfully.

"Saffron," Ma sounded serious. "In a few minutes we are going to have a solemn and important talk with our children. Would you please see to it that no one from the village eavesdrops? Warn us if anyone should approach."

"Certainly, Mistress," Saffron fluttered her moth-like wings. "You may rely on me," and the fairy vanished.

Breakfast was on the table, but even for Ma's beautiful fresh bread and Mistress Alice's honey, the children had none of their usual appetite. Emmet felt as though he had a leaden weight in his stomach, preventing anything from going down. Normally Ma would not have allowed them to leave a crumb, but today she seemed not to see the wasted food that they pushed listlessly around their platters.

When all had been cleared away, to the great surprise and delight of Bessie the goat, grateful recipient of all household waste, each child held a mug of warm milk and Pa began to speak.

"It seems to me," he began slowly, "that there is much we need to explain to you all. As you learned yesterday, we are not an ordinary family. You have heard something of my history. Favoured by the Gods for my skill as a smith, I have lived many years beyond my allotted span, never growing any physically older than I appear to you now. I have had other wives, other families in past centuries, but they are not immortal, and each must live out their life times and pass into the arms of the Great Mother, even as you will do when your time comes. My gift from the Gods is both a blessing and a curse."

Pa gazed at each child in turn. No one spoke. He continued.

"Your mother is the seventh daughter of a seventh daughter. Her mother, who was a great lady, taught her the Craft, for she knew she had inherited the power."

He glanced at Ma who took up the tale.

"You children also have the power, although you are not aware of it, and I have not yet begun to teach you.

"We live in dangerous times, the burning times, as the Silver Hare said. Those who serve the Great Mother are no longer honoured and revered as her priestesses, but feared and hated as witches."

She said the word with difficulty, as though it was painful to her tongue.

"There is much we have hidden from you in order that you might have a safe and normal childhood, and I would have hoped to have left it longer, at least until Lily was a good bit older."

Lily, thumb plugged firmly in her mouth, had a white milk moustache rising above it.

"It is difficult to be aware of the world of faery, to have powers that others do not have, to own the ability to cast spells, heal the sick and shape-shift, without letting others know about it. In order to survive, we had to practise many deceptions."

"You mean," said Letty, light beginning to dawn, "you could have cured Emmet's spots yourself?"

Ma nodded apologetically. "I could."

"And Pa didn't need to have his blood let!" Emmet was outraged.

"No, I'm afraid he didn't."

Hetty was white-faced.

"Charlie, Will, John, Janie and Rosie!" she said. "You let them die!"

Ma's eyes filled with tears, which trickled slowly down her face. She didn't answer. Pa spoke for her.

"We do not have the right to transgress the natural laws, sweetheart. Ma used all her healing powers. They died because it was written that they would. Their time had come."

Hetty put her arms around Ma.

"I'm sorry," she whispered into her mother's neck. "I shouldn't have said that. I'm so sorry, Ma."

Lily took her thumb out, with its customary pop.

"Ma," she said, thoughtfully, "can you see them? Their ghosts I mean?"

Ma looked at Lily through her tears.

"No child, it takes a special power to see the spirits of the dead, and it is not something I have ever tried to invoke. Why do you ask?"

"Well," said Lily, "Emmet wished it. He wished he wasn't the oldest and he wasn't. They came, you see. Ooh, it was lovely! Janie wears my stone with the hole in it. We all danced! Rosie loves my feather. But they can't eat, poor things. And then Hetty wished, and you and Pa must have been just coming, so I'spect you can see them too!"

"Lily," said Pa, "what on earth are you talking about?"

Emmet came to Lily's rescue and the whole story came tumbling out – the Holy Well, the magic potion, the wishes, the Wild Hunt – everything.

"And then you came to find us," he finished, simply.

Ma began to cry all over again.

"Ma," Letty was distressed, "I thought it would make you happy!"

"Oh, Letty," said Ma through her tears, "oh, sweetheart, I am happy. If only you knew, to see my darlings again, what a joy that would be."

Lily climbed up onto Ma's knee, wound chubby arms around her mother's neck, and planted a milky kiss on her cheek. Ma rocked her for a moment, like a baby, and then gently put Lily down and wiped her eyes.

"So many secrets we have between us. Now that you know your true heritage, I must begin to teach you the craft. But everything you learn must be a secret. I cannot stress to you enough how important this is. No one outside the Company of the Silver Hare must ever suspect that the Smith family is anything other than ordinary. If you see a member of the fairy clans when an outsider is present, never look at them or acknowledge them in any way. This is not easy to do, but it is something you must master – your lives depend upon it! Likewise, when I teach you to shape shift, you must never change unless you are certain you are alone."

Ma looked at the children in turn. They gazed back at her solemnly, although Hetty and Letty could both feel a bubble of excitement rising inside themselves – they were to learn spells, and shape shifting!

"Lily," Ma put her arm around her youngest daughter. "You will have to be so careful. I know how you love to chatter, but you must beware. You have seen a hanging, haven't you?"

Lily gave a shudder and nodded.

"Yes, Ma. It was horrible."

"Well, sweetheart," Ma looked searchingly into her eyes. "I never, never, want that to happen to any of you. Do you understand?"

Lily's eyes looked ready to pop out of her head.

"Yes Ma!"

60

"Also," said Ma, "I know how fond you are of Jennet and Jimmy, but you must not openly appear too friendly with them. When the finger of blame is pointed, it must not point in this direction."

Emmet's heart sunk. Not to be friends with Jennet! He and the twins exchanged unhappy glances. Pa caught the looks.

"However," he said thoughtfully, "perhaps I can see a way around the difficulty. The Demdikes are poor. Ma could do with a maid to help with the work here, even with you three girls there's a lot to do. I could use a boy in the forge. It would be a charity to take two children from a poor family particularly if one is said to be half-witted, give them good food and a chance in life. They could live-in here and visit their family on Sundays."

"That is a clever idea, Master Smith. Surely there will be rewards in heaven for a comfortably off family to extend alms to those who are not so fortunate as themselves. And to make it above suspicion, do not approach Mistress Demdike directly. Rather, do you lay the plan first before the vicar. He is bound to approve and shall arrange it all."

Jennet to live with them always. It was so wonderful, he could scarcely believe it.

"Oh, Ma," Lily was thrilled. "Jimmy is my best person in all the world. Can Henny Penny sleep in our bed with us?"

7. The Initiation

And so it was arranged. The vicar was happy to be party to removing a pair of innocents from what he viewed as a rather disreputable family, and as Ma foretold, praised the admirable charity of the Smiths.

"Although how much help that boy will be you, I couldn't say," he remarked to Pa in a tone of sorrowful complacence. "James seems to be completely witless. Watch out that he doesn't burn the forge down by mistake, or worse," he added. "There are certain rumours about Old Demdike... one can't be too careful." He glanced about him and lowered his voice. "Witchcraft, you know."

Pa contrived to look suitably shocked and murmured blandly that he was too busy himself to listen to idle gossip but would be quite certain to stand for no nonsense.

"I shall give him a sound thrashing every Sunday," said Master Smith earnestly. "That will keep the devil away."

"Excellent." The vicar was appreciative. "Exactly what I would do myself, under the circumstances. They will have a good home with you. Be certain to work them as hard as you can. Satan makes work for idle hands, you know. And don't overfeed them. Avoid red meat."

Ma gave a snort of laughter which she hurriedly turned into a cough. Pa had never so much as raised a hand to any of his children in their lives, and to hear him talk of beating the small and gentle Jimmy was too much for her. The vicar looked at her in surprise.

"A tickle," she said, by way of explanation. "I shall give them bread and water. And I shall beat Jennet every Thursday."

Her face twitched uncontrollably. "Do excuse me, vicar. I must go and stir the stew."

She rushed into the cottage and shut the door firmly.

"It is all arranged, then." The vicar adjusted the brim of his hat. "I will bring them to you tomorrow."

62

Jennet and Jimmy arrived the next morning. Each clutched a small bundle of possessions. Jimmy, as always, held Henny Penny under his arm.

"Here they are." The vicar pushed them both towards Ma. "The boy insisted on bringing the hen. I doubt it will lay, it seems rather old, but if you wring its neck you might get a meal or two out of it. You'll need to boil it well. Old hens are rather tough, my housekeeper says."

There was a horrified silence, broken by Henny Penny who let out an outraged squawk.

"Thank you Vicar," said Ma hastily. "I'll take them now and deal with the hen. So good of you to take so much trouble. Good day to you."

She dropped a curtsey and pushed Jennet and Jimmy into the cottage with one fluid movement.

Lily was furious.

"How could that horrible old man talk about cooking Henny Penny? He's cruel and I hate him!"

Henny Penny had recovered her composure.

"It's alright, Lily. He doesn't know who he is talking about. Too old to lay! I'll show him."

She laid an egg neatly on the hearth and another on the cushion of Ma's rocking chair.

"These aren't special ones. You can eat these for supper. Here, have some more."

She laid one in the wood basket and another in Pa's Sunday hat.

Ma gathered them up and placed them in a blue bowl on the dresser.

"We are honoured and delighted to have you under our humble roof."

She made a curtsey to Henny Penny who inclined her red-combed head graciously.

"We are grateful for any eggs you care to lay us, although of course you are under no obligation. However, if you do feel so moved, would you mind doing it in this basket?"

Ma set a rush basket down beside the hearth. It was a good

size, softly lined with a rabbit skin.

"I should hate to waste any of your precious eggs, and if you lay them all over the place, they might be accidentally broken. Also, you may find this a comfortable place to rest."

Henny Penny, completely mollified, inspected her new basket appreciatively.

"Acceptable, Mistress Smith, very acceptable indeed. I thank you kindly. If you will all excuse me."

She stepped in, settling herself comfortably, put her head under her wing and went to sleep. Ma turned to Jennet and Jimmy.

"My dears, we are so happy to have you with us. Twins, take Jennet upstairs and show her where she can put her things. Emmet, you show Jimmy the loft. Come back when you are ready and we will have a posset and gingerbread."

The girls clattered up the stairs, except for Lily who had firmly attached herself to Jimmy, following him and Emmet into the forge. Jennet looked around the tiny bedroom with delight.

"This is so pretty," she said.

Pa had made a box bed for her which fitted against the wall, covered with a gay, patchwork quilt. It had a tiny shelf for a candlestick with her name carved on the headboard. There was an oak cupboard and a chest along one wall for clothes, with a jug and basin on top of it and a stone jar full of roses. Bunches of lavender hung from the beams and there was a sheepskin on the floor between the two beds by way of a rug. On the windowsill was Saffron, sunbathing in her usual spot. Lily had thoughtfully gathered some sheep's wool to make a mattress for her. She looked up as the girls entered.

"Jennet!" She fluttered off the windowsill and perched on the end of the bed. "How lovely to see you! Lily has been excited about you coming."

"We all have," said Letty. "Wasn't it a good idea of Pa's?"

Jennet sat down on her new bed and drew her knees up to her chin.

"It's not good at home right now. We were glad to come

away." She picked at the quilt. "Granny and Ma are upset about what Aunt Salome saw." She spoke with some difficulty. "They keep fighting about it. Ma says it's all Granny's fault and Granny blames Old Chattox. Then Old Chattox came round and blamed Granny. They fought, and now none of them speak to each other. They cry a lot too."

The twins sat on each side of Jennet, and each put an arm around her in silent sympathy. They didn't know what to say. Saffron broke the silence.

"Are you frightened, Jennet?" she asked.

Jennet regarded her for a moment with her bright green eyes.

"No," she said firmly, "I'm not."

"Not even," Letty felt awkward saying it, "of being hanged?"

"I'm not going to be hanged!" Jennet spoke with conviction. "None of us are. The Silver Hare won't let that happen. And anyway, I wished..."

"What did you wish?" Letty asked eagerly.

"I can't tell you yet." Jennet was mysterious. "I will tell you one day, I promise, when it comes true."

Hetty was puzzled. "But all our wishes came true straight away. Why won't yours?"

"It's the sort of wish that takes time," which was all she would say about it.

Saffron curled up on her mattress again and closed her eyes.

"Wake me up if anything exciting happens," she murmured, sleepily. The twins giggled. She was the most lazy fairy. All she seemed to do was sleep in the sun, like a cat.

"Come on, Jennet," said Hetty, "let's go down and have our posset."

The rest of the day was spent settling in. Jennet and Jimmy were delighted with the new arrangement and both proved to be extremely helpful. Jennet was like quicksilver, fast and able at whatever she was asked to do, and Jimmy, despite his strange appearance and simple speech, was far from being stupid.

After supper, Pa carefully bolted the cottage door and asked everyone to come through the side into the forge. The children were puzzled but obediently followed him. He shut and bolted that door, and the large, front one used by customers. Ma went to the window and murmured the charm.

"Are we ready?" Pa asked her.

"We are," she said. "I've charmed the window so no one can look in, and as an extra precaution, I've asked Figwort to stand guard. He likes doing that," she said, "it makes him feel important."

Pa pulled out some benches, and bid the children sit down.

"We are just waiting for a visitor and then we can begin," he said. "Ah, I think she may have arrived."

There was a sound of loud scuffling in the bread oven. The iron door, which was ajar, burst open, and out struggled an elderly raven, bedraggled, in a cloud of soot. It hopped to the floor, gave a bad-tempered cough, and to the astonishment of the Smith children, abruptly turned itself into Old Demdike.

"Hello Granny."

Jennet seemed unsurprised and got up politely to give her grandmother a kiss.

"Don't touch me child, you'll get filthy. Damn chimney wants sweeping!"

She glared at Pa who bowed politely.

"Greetings Mistress. I apologise for the soot. The fire in the oven is rarely out long enough to sweep it. Would you take a glass of methyglyn?"

Old Demdike brightened visibly and spat some soot onto the floor.

"That would touch the spot," she admitted grudgingly, and took the pewter mug that Pa offered her, seating herself in a large wooden chair. She took a deep draught and wiped her mouth with the back of her hand. Soot smeared itself across her face and Hetty gave a stifled squeak. Ma gave her a pained look, and Jennet jabbed her hard in the ribs. Old Demdike took out her clay pipe and began to pack it with tobacco.

"So," she said, lighting it deftly, "you young 'uns are to learn the craft. Now there's a fine thing, to be sure."

"It is indeed." Ma looked serious. "Your Jennet and James have been taught quite a bit already, I know, but I thought all the children might have lessons together. They need to learn to protect themselves before..." Her voice faltered. "...before the next Lammas tide."

Old Demdike nodded slowly.

"True enough, true enough," she agreed.

Emmet noticed a pulse flicker in her temple. Pa got up from the bench and took his great bellows into his hands. He went over to the fire of his furnace, which almost never went out but which was burning low, as the day's work was done. He applied the bellows and a shower of sparks shot up the chimney. The flames began to shoot higher and higher, casting strange patterns on the walls and ceiling of the cave-like forge. When the humming began, Emmet realised that he was expecting it.

A familiar shape began to form in the heart of the flames. As the humming stopped, the Silver Hare stepped delicately out of the furnace into the centre of the forge. Emmet could feel the heat of the flames emitting from its body. It looked at the company in silence for a moment. The only sound was the crackling of flames and the puffing of Old Demdike at her pipe.

"Greetings," said the Silver Hare. "You young ones," and it gazed around at the children as it spoke, "are about to take your first faltering steps on the path of the Great Mother. This is a wonderful thing, and no light matter. Those who learn the Old Ways, the ways of magic and hidden things, carry a great burden of responsibility. Those initiated into the Company of the Silver Hare are sworn to use their powers only for good. Any who step off the path into darkness, even for a moment, put themselves at great risk."

Its luminous eyes seemed to rest on Old Demdike for the briefest of seconds and Emmet thought that the look it gave her was one of tender pity. Old Demdike went on sucking her

67

pipe and would not meet its gaze.

"So, children," it continued, "tonight you shall all make a solemn promise, and you shall also receive a gift."

It turned to Ma.

"Mistress Smith, will you cast a circle?"

Ma obediently called in the four directions and trod the circle widdershins around the gathering. Once again, bread, wine and salt were crumbled, and everyone took a mouthful.

"Now children, you must each most solemnly swear on earth, on water, on fire and on air, on the body of the Great Mother, that you will never knowingly use your powers for harm."

Each child in turn gave their solemn promise, Emmet faltering over the words, but small Lily shouting them out with great relish. The Silver Hare gave her a look of fond amusement.

"Well done, sister!" it said. "Well done all of you. And now for the gifts. Wayland?"

Pa stepped forward bearing his silver breastplate like a tray. He held it out to the children. Inside, nestling in a piece of green silk, were five tiny Silver Hares, just like the one that Lily wore around her neck. There was a murmur of delight.

"Take one each," urged the Silver Hare. "You, child," he said to Lily, "have yours already. Wear them always, with pride and with reverence. Show them to any other member of the Company and they are bound to help you."

"Also," it added, "in times of great danger or trouble, you have only to ask, and they will bring you home. And now, let the secret initiation begin."

8. A NIGHT AT THE GRAVEYARD

It was a fine July evening. The heat of the day was giving way to the cooler air of the dusk. The evening star hung brightly like a single lamp in the indigo of a cloudless sky. The churchyard drowsed silently. Rabbits nibbled the turf around the edges of the old gravestones and a thrush sang its heart out in the branches of a lilac tree. A small fairy alighted on the ancient stone wall that formed a boundary and looked keenly around her.

"Any humans about?" she enquired of the thrush.

"At this time of day?" The thrush was amused. "Not likely! They are too afraid of ghosts," and it carried on with its song.

The fairy put two fingers into her dainty mouth and let out an astonishingly loud whistle for one so small.

"All clear!" she called.

Eight pairs of long furry ears appeared above the dry stone wall, followed by the sinewy agile bodies of brown hares, a large male, a smaller female, and six young ones. They leaped the wall and, as they touched the grass of the churchyard, turned into the entire Smith family, accompanied by Jennet and Jimmy.

"Well done children!" Pa was approving. "Neatly done. Timing was excellent. Emmet, I think you've got it now."

It was exactly a month since the children had been initiated into the company of the Silver Hare. Ma, as good as her word, had taught them many things. The twins were quick to learn, and Jennet and Jimmy knew much already. Lily, to everyone's surprise, showed real brilliance, but for Emmet it was a slow and painful process, and of all the lessons they had learned, shape shifting was the one which he found the most challenging.

"You must think like a hare," Ma urged, "feel it in your bones and in your blood. That's right. Oh dear!"

Some part of Emmet always seemed to remain obstinately

un-hare-like or, if he lost concentration, would turn into something quite unexpected, like the time he was distracted by a passing frog and ended up part hare, part amphibian. The twins had teased him mercilessly, but Jennet, who never mocked him no matter how badly he got it wrong, gave him extra lessons at night in the forge, with a sleepy Saffron standing guard outside, until at last he had mastered it.

They were longing to take Ma and Pa to the churchyard at night to see their departed siblings, but Ma said that it would be too risky until they could shape-shift perfectly.

"If anyone sees us, they'll think we're… you know," she said, "gathering skulls, or some such nonsense."

"You mean witches, Ma, don't you?" Lily asked.

"Don't say that word." Ma was severe. "It's not a good word, it's not a nice word and it isn't what we are. Don't use it again Lily."

Once Emmet was proficient enough to undertake the journey to the churchyard, the company set out from the forge, as though for an evening stroll. Jennet and Jimmy maintained a respectable distance behind as befitting their station as servants. When they were well out of sight of the village, Ma stopped.

"This is a good place to change," she said. "I have put a spell of forgetfulness on the village which will last until noon tomorrow. If anyone saw us walking out this evening or sees us return tomorrow, they will not remember. Hetty, what is the first thing to do when you change?"

"Make absolutely sure no one sees you." said Hetty, smartly.

"Jennet, what happens if you are injured whilst you are changed?"

"Get home if it's safe to do so," Jennet answered.

Then she asked Emmet the most terrible question of all.

"Emmet, what happens if you are killed?"

He swallowed uncomfortably.

"You turn back into yourself."

"That's right." Ma looked around at them all severely. "So

that must never happen. What if you are injured and can't get home, Lily?"

"Use your Silver Hare amulet. But Ma, we know all this. Can't we just change? I want to go!"

Pa spoke patiently. "It is because we are so careful, that no finger of suspicion has ever been pointed at us, Lily. This is why we only shape-shift if it is necessary. If you can't take it seriously, then perhaps you should go home to the forge and wait with Henny Penny."

Lily was horrified. "Sorry Pa, please don't make me go home! I will be careful."

Pa looked at Ma who nodded. "Check once more – no one is about, everyone has their amulets – good. Now, CHANGE!"

All was silent but for the singing thrush.

"We shall walk the boundary," said Ma, "and set a repelling charm."

Hetty and Letty rolled their eyes at each other behind Ma's back, but they followed her obediently enough. Ma led the way, widdershins, around the perimeter of the old stonewall, stopping at north, south, east and west to call in the directions. All the time, a blue dusk was gathering. Emmet could feel the heat radiating from the sun-warmed stones. A delicate mist began to rise from the quiet grass.

"Listen!"

Jennet stopped short and Emmet, close behind, bumped into her. A faint rustling sound, like dry leaves in the wind, rippled through the graveyard. Emmet thought he could hear a faint murmuring. He gave Jennet a questioning look. "It's the Dead," said Jennet quietly. "They are waking."

Up from the graves there rose a host of shapes, vague and indeterminate at first, then clearer.

"Look," Letty whispered to Hetty, "it's old Mrs. Law that died last year in the cholera epidemic! And there's old Seth the cowman. Do you remember, Pa said he drank himself to death?"

Old Mrs. Law shook out her grave-clothes tidily and settled herself comfortably against a gravestone. Up from the

71

earth floated two tiny shapes that formed into newborn babies. Mrs. Law caught them deftly in her withered arms and rocked them gently.

"There now, there now, my pretties, granny's got you, so she has."

She began to croon a lullaby, and the babies nestled against her contentedly.

"Come on," said Emmet, "let's find Charlie and the others. Their graves are there, in the middle."

They picked their way between the gravestones where it was getting busy. Men, women and children were popping up all over the place. One small boy emerged right between Emmet's feet.

"Oy!" he said indignantly. "That's my grave you're standing on. Watch where you're going. Oh, hello Emmet!"

Emmet recognised him as Billy, a friend from the village who had drowned in Pendle Water two summers ago.

"Hello Billy," he said. "It's good to see you again."

"You too Emmet," said Billy. "I'm glad you are here. There's something I wanted to tell you." Emmet thought that Billy might have something wonderful to tell him about heaven, but instead, Billy said, "You know when someone stole that pie your ma baked, the one she left out to cool and she blamed you, so you got no supper and a good walloping?" Emmet remembered it well. "It was me," said Billy. "I'm sorry, Emmet. I was going to own up when I heard you got into trouble but I got drowned before I had the chance."

"That's alright," said Emmet. "I guessed it was you. I never told on you, I just missed having you to play with. You could own up now, though. Ma's here somewhere. I guess she can't wallop you, now you're a ghost."

"She still scares me though," said Billy.

"Nobody seems surprised that we are here," remarked Letty, "or that we can see you."

"We've been expecting you," said Billy. "Charlie told us all about it. We were surprised you didn't come sooner. They've been looking out for you every night."

72

They had almost reached the centre of the graveyard. Lily was looking about eagerly.

"Rosie!" she called. "Ro-sie! Where are you? It's me, Lily."

"Wait!" Jennet grabbed her by the arm and pointed.

Seated on the grass were Ma and Pa, Ma's green gown making an odd splash of colour amongst the greys and whites. Ma rocked Rosie in her arms, their cheeks pressed close together. Janie sat on Pa's knee, laughing with delight and Charlie, John and Will knelt behind with their arms around as much of their parents as they could manage. Tears were pouring down Ma's face and yet she seemed happy. Pa too, had tears in his eyes. Emmet had never seen his Pa cry before.

"Come on," said Jennet, "this is your Ma and Pa's special time. Let's leave them a while. Don't let's spoil it for them. Come on Lily."

The children backed away quietly and, dodging between some tall gravestones, interrupted a pair of ghostly lovers, embracing.

"Do you mind?" The woman tossed her grave-bleached hair and a small worm dropped onto Emmet's foot. He kicked if off hastily and they moved on.

"She died on her wedding day," said Billy, "poor thing. Then he died of a broken heart. Now they are together forever. They're always kissing, though. Ugh!"

The part of the graveyard the children now found themselves in seemed older and overgrown, as though there was no one left alive to tend the graves of the people buried there. The mist was thicker and there was a strange atmosphere, not quite a smell, not quite a feeling.

"Old magic," Jennet whispered. "I wonder…"

"We don't come up this end much," said Billy, uneasily. "The Old Ones are buried here. They don't mix with the rest of us and they don't like to be disturbed. I think we should go back," and he vanished in a skirl of mist.

"Well, well!"

A deep voice made them jump. The mist receded to reveal

a dark figure, swathed in a black coat. Starlight glinted on gold-hoop earrings.

"Aunt Salome Boswell!" Lily beamed at her. "What are you doing here? Have you got dead friends, too?"

The Chovihani regarded them unsmilingly. Two more figures appeared behind her, the tall elf Atterlothe and Figwort the gnome.

"Greetings, children of The Five," said Atterlothe. He winked at Emmet. "It's busy here tonight. Anyone would think it was All Hallows Eve."

The overgrown ground in front of them began to tremble a little and the children could just see the outline of three mounds, barely visible beneath the undergrowth. Out from the graves, slowly, like blind moles emerging from their tunnels, came three ancient ghosts, so worn and tattered there barely seemed any substance to them.

"Who calls us?" the first said, in a hoarse and windy voice. "Who calls us from our deathly sleep?"

As they fully emerged from the graves, the children could see that the ghosts were three ancient women, stooped and skinny, almost bald and completely toothless.

"Well?" the second spoke querulously. "It had better be good. We like our sleep."

"Who wakes us?" demanded the third. Her voice was stronger and younger than the others. "Who comes and disturbs the Demdike Sisters? Speak up!"

"Demdike!" Hetty whispered to Jennet excitedly. "That's your name!" Jennet and Jimmy exchanged unhappy glances. Jimmy spoke firmly.

"We go now. Back to your Ma and Pa. Not our business here. Come on my Lily. Come Hetty, Letty."

"But Jimmy," Letty was puzzled, "they might be your great-great-great-something grannies. Don't you want to talk to them?"

Aunt Salome Boswell shot the children an angry look.

"Go now!" she hissed fiercely. "The Brother is right. This is not your business, nor is it a good place. Go quickly. Has

74

not your mother taught you to obey without question one of The Five?"

"I'll deal with them." Figwort spoke in his usual important manner. "Come on all of you. It's all right, you haven't done anything wrong, but you need to go now."

He half-ushered, half-shooed them back the way they had come. Jennet's face wore the wooden expression that meant she was keeping her own counsel. The Smith children were bewildered. Emmet cast one swift look back over his shoulder and heard Aunt Salome Boswell speak to the ancient ones.

"It is I, the Chovihani of the Company of the Silver Hare. I wake you to enlist your help in a matter of utmost importance…" then they were out of earshot.

"Lily!" Rosie rushed towards them, delighted. "Where have you been? Come and play. There's lots of your old friends here, desperate to see you. Come on!"

Living and dead child scampered off, hand in hand. Hetty and Letty followed with Jennet. Ma was sitting where they had left her, holding Charlie's hand, Will leaning against her shoulder and John lying with his head in her lap. Emmet thought that he had never seen her look so happy. Pa stood beside them, deep in conversation with Charlie.

"There you are," said Pa, contentedly. "We wondered where you'd all got to. Come and spend some time with your brothers, Emmet. We can't stay too much longer."

"A few more hours, Wayland." Ma's voice was pleading."

Pa dropped a kiss on the top of her head.

"A few more hours then. We will come again you know."

Ma nodded. Her eyes followed her daughters, racing around the gravestones in a wild game of tag, dodging in and out, screaming with laughter. Janie dashed up to them.

"Come on, you three, come and play. It's better with more people."

She rushed off again, but not fast enough to avoid being 'tagged' by Rosie. Emmet looked tentatively at Jennet. She still seemed troubled, but as she caught his eye, her face softened.

75

"Come on," she said, grabbing both him and Jimmy by the hands. "We only have a few hours left – let's make the most of it."

9. Liquid Life Force

When they reached home, it was business as usual in the Smithy, even though they had been up all night. Lily, especially, was exhausted, but Ma would not allow anyone to sleep.

"If we are all in bed, people will wonder." she said, firmly. "You can all have an early night tonight. Go and feed Bessie, please Lily, and do stop whining."

They did all go to bed early, but the tiredness persisted for more than a week with everyone looking desperately pale. Saffron grew worried about them and disappeared one morning to return late in the evening accompanied by Atterlothe. He came in with his usual easy manner, hanging his cloak on the back of the door then bowing in a courtly manner.

"Greetings, Master Smith, Mistress!" His keen eyes gave them a penetrating look. "You are all unwell," he began gently. "More tired than you should be. And your thoughts, I think, turn always to those who are gone from you, who lie buried in the churchyard. Am I not right?"

Pa raised an eyebrow. "And if you are?"

Atterlothe sighed. "There is a reason why humans should not seek the dead. I think you need reminding of it. Too much time with them and they draw from your life force. They cannot help it, and the more they draw, the more like them you become. The more like them you become, the more you wish to be with them. There are only two nights of the year when the natural laws are suspended - St John's Eve and All Hallows Eve."

Pa nodded slowly. Ma looked stricken. Atterlothe put a gentle hand on her arm.

"You miss them so much, I know. A mother's love reaches beyond the grave. But you should not break the natural laws. It is not long until Halloween. Do not take your family into danger again. Look, I bring you this."

77

From the leather bag that hung from his waist, he produced a small crystal bottle.

"It is a magic tonic. Liquid life force, the elvish folk call it. A drop each in mead, morning and night, until it is gone. You will soon be restored."

Ma took the bottle from him, un-stoppered it and sniffed.

"Valerian," she said, "and garlic. What else?"

Atterlothe grinned. "Faery secrets!" he said. "Surely you have secret ingredients in your potions, Mistress?"

Ma's face relaxed. "I do. Thank you for your kindness, Atterlothe. We shall heed your warning. And we shall drink the tonic."

Pa pulled out a bench draped in sheepskin.

"Come and bide with us a while and share a pipe of tobacco with me."

Atterlothe sat down and took out a long clay pipe. Ma poured mead for everyone and added drops from the crystal bottle. As he sipped his, Emmet felt a golden, glowing warmth spreading deep within him.

"Oh," said Lily, "it's lovely. I've got life force in my tummy. Can I have some more?"

"In the morning," said Atterlothe. "Enough is as good as a feast."

Ma and the girls got out their straw filled lace cushions and in no time at all their bobbins were clicking away. They had felt too tired to work at them lately, but with the potion coursing through their veins, they felt infused with energy. Jennet had her own cushion now, and Emmet had slowly and painstakingly whittled her some lace bobbins. They were rough compared to the ones Pa made, but Jennet was delighted with them, and her first piece of lace was growing in a most encouraging fashion.

Jimmy sat by the hearth with his arms around Henny Penny. Lily knelt beside him dressing her rag doll made by Ma from old scraps of cloth. It had sheep's wool sewn on for hair and an embroidered face, grubby from much cuddling. Lily called it 'Mistress Mary' and loved it. It was the first time she had played with it for a long time as so many exciting things had been happening. As Mistress Mary was kept under Lily's bed in a box, Jennet had never made her acquaintance before. She looked up from her lace making and saw the doll for the first time.

"Oh, Lily!" she exclaimed, without thinking. "She's just like the dolls Granny makes!"

Jimmy turned a warning look at his sister, but it was too late. The atmosphere in the room was at once electric.

"Jennet!" Atterlothe looked stern. His voice was as cold as ice. "Has your grandmother been making poppets?"

Every eye was turned on Jennet. She blushed as red as her hair and burst into tears. Pa looked grave.

"Someone has indeed stepped off the path into the darkness," he said quietly.

The Smith children were bewildered. Something was clearly wrong, but they could make no sense of it.

"What is it?" asked Emmet tentatively, after the silence had grown painful. "Why can't Jennet's Granny make dolls? Is it bad?"

Atterlothe spoke heavily.

"When a witch," he spat the word deliberately, "makes a doll or a poppet, she makes it in the likeness of the person she wishes to harm. She sticks pins in it where she wishes to hurt them. Then she hides it away and that person suffers agonies. She can remove the pins and stop the suffering, or she can burn it and the person will die."

"Did you know about this, Henny Penny?" asked Ma.

"No," said Henny Penny. "I would not have remained in the Demdike household had I known. I swear on the Silver Hare that this is true."

"She didn't know," Jennet sobbed. "Only I knew, and I told Jimmy. I saw Granny one night through a crack in the door. I didn't understand what she was doing but I knew it was bad. She never saw me. I crept back to bed. Please don't tell the Silver Hare. Please don't get my Granny into trouble."

She burst into even louder sobs. Ma put aside her lace-making cushion and lifted Jennet onto her knee. She rocked her gently and stroked her wild red hair, but Jennet was inconsolable.

"Jennet," said Pa, kindly, "don't cry any more. What is done is done. Your Granny is already in more trouble than anyone else could get her into. We will have to tell the Silver Hare. Old Demdike has knowingly broken the law of the Great Mother and she must abide by the consequences."

Jennet sat up, tearful and anxious.

"Will she be punished?" she asked, piteously. "What will the Silver Hare do?"

"That remains to be seen," said Atterlothe, grimly. "It is now only a week until Lammas and the Company will meet again at Roughlee Hall. Until then, we will do nothing."

He looked at Jennet's poor, swollen face and softened.

"Don't upset yourself, sweetheart," he said. "It is not your fault, and your Granny's sins would have found her out sooner or later. Indeed, now we know the rhyme and reason of the troubles which are yet to come. Good will come of this so do not grieve. I must go now. I bid you all goodnight. Until Lammastide."

Ma made Jennet a posset of poppy, chamomile and mandragore to help her sleep deeply. In the morning, she was pale but more composed. The rest of the week seemed to pass extra slowly. Pa would not allow Jennet and Jimmy to visit their home before Lammas and sent a message with Saffron to say that they were too busy at the forge and could not be spared at present. Everyone was kind to Jennet, but it was extremely difficult to get a smile out of her. Jimmy, who always spoke little, was silent. The cottage seemed as though a shadow had been cast over it, despite the liquid life force.

Ma cleaned the cottage from top to bottom and had all the girls busily weeding the herb garden. Henny Penny was given some of the potion even though she hadn't been to the graveyard. She began to lay eggs at such a rate that Ma could hardly keep up with her and sent Lily with a basketful to take round to some of the old folk of the village. Pa, Emmet and

Jimmy worked long hours in the forge, and the furnace burned brightly far into the night.

In the fields around the village, the corn was ripening, and all the men were busy bringing in the harvest. Halfway through the week, Pa took the boys out into the fields with scythes to lend a hand. The weather was glorious and the air was filled with golden dust from the cutting of the corn which got into ears, noses and throats. Ma and the girls carried out great pitchers of mead and ale for the haymakers and then joined the women in gleaning whatever corn was missed by them.

In such ways they kept themselves busy until, at last, it was the Eve of Lammas.

10. The Feast of Lammas

Ma woke them all early with the smell of new bread baking in the forge. The loaves she had made were first of the new-ground corn, twisted and plaited to resemble sheaves. She had created a magnificent corn dolly from the last stook to be harvested, with ears of corn for its hair and wide skirts, all bedecked with ribbons. It was seated on the settle by the hearth in the cottage. Lily eyed it longingly.

"Can't I play with her, Ma? I'd be so careful."

Ma shook her head firmly.

"She's not a toy, Lily. Don't dare touch her." But seeing her daughter's crestfallen expression, she softened. "I'll make you one of your own, if you are good."

"Oh, thank you Ma!" Lily was delighted. "I'll be just as good as I can be."

The whole household was seated around the table, breakfasting on herbed scrambled eggs and the last of the old bread. Jennet felt terrible. It had been the longest and most difficult week of her short life. She felt wracked with guilt and anxiety about giving away Old Demdike, and now the day had dawned when she would have to face her grandmother with the Company of the Silver Hare. She did not know how she would be able to bear it. Her stomach tied itself in knots, and butterflies looped the loop inside it relentlessly.

Emmet, sitting next to her, noticed that she wasn't eating, and felt desperately sorry for her. He took her hand under the table and squeezed it. Her small fingers seemed lifeless, as cold as ice despite the warmth of the morning. Ma rose from the table and began to clear the dishes.

"Lily, go and wash your face, you've got honey all over it. Hetty and Letty, please do each other's hair and then Lily's. Jennet, pack the basket. Jimmy, collect the eggs - we'll take some to Mistress Alice. Emmet, feed Bessie and then we can set off. We go in our own forms today. There is no need to use magic for the sake of it."

82

Pa gave Emmet a humorous look and a wink and went outside to smoke his pipe whilst preparations were made. Once the whole household was assembled outside the forge, they set off in the direction of Roughlee Hall.

The air was golden and dusty from the recent haymaking, red poppies flourished in the hedgerows whilst the sky was full of the sound of riotous birdsong. The Demdike children were completely unaware, however, of the beauty of the day. They plodded along, staring straight in front of them with unseeing eyes, their faces set and grim. Even Henny Penny, tucked under Jimmy's arm as usual, had nothing to say.

It seemed to Emmet to be a much longer walk than he remembered. Ma and Pa chatted brightly of this and that, but all the children were affected by Jennet's unhappiness and eventually lapsed into silence. It was almost a relief when the Hall hove into view, lying quietly in the warm sunshine, stately and unchanged as always.

"Surely nothing bad could ever happen in this lovely place?" Emmet thought to himself.

Mistress Alice met them at the front gate.

"Come inside, my dears," she said. "The Company shall meet before the celebrations today, and what takes place shall determine what will be left to celebrate."

She spoke lightly, but her eyes were sombre, and Emmet felt a lurch of fear in his stomach.

They entered through the front door this time, which somehow made the occasion seem more solemn, and Mistress Alice led them into the familiar dining chamber. The Smith family was the last of the company to arrive. Ma and the girls made deep curtseys to the Silver Hare whilst Pa and Emmet bowed low.

"Welcome." The Silver Hare greeted them in its starry voice. "Come and be seated."

The thrones of The Five had been brought in and Ma seated herself on the right of the Silver Hare. The children found seats opposite, on the other side of the great oak table. Old Demdike, already in her place on the Hare's left, saw

Jennet's look of white faced misery, and cast her a piercing glance, but Jennet avoided her gaze. As before, all the Faery Clans were represented, and Atterlothe sat beside Wayland Smith. He gave Jennet a glance of concern. She held Jimmy's hand so tightly that her fingers showed white at the knuckles, and she looked almost as if she might faint. Indeed, she felt sick and dizzy with fear, and a cold sweat showed clammy on her forehead. Atterlothe made a decision.

"My Lord," he addressed the Silver Hare, "have I your permission to speak? There is something of great import I must lay before the Company which has much relevance to the position in which we find ourselves."

The Silver Hare inclined its head.

"Speak my good friend. You have our full attention."

Atterlothe took a deep breath. He did not look at old Demdike.

"It has come to the painful notice of some of our number that a member of our Company has stepped knowingly from the light into the darkness. This, I believe, is the root of the troubles that we know are to come."

There was a brief silence that was broken by the horrible sound of Jennet being violently sick. The twins gasped in shock and disbelief, and Lily's eyes were round with sympathy. To be sick in front of the Silver Hare! They were hard put to think of anything more outrageous or humiliating. Mistress Alice moved quickly.

"Anne," she called in a calm voice, "a bowl of water and a cloth, if you please. And my smelling salts and some oil of lavender. Our sister has been taken ill."

She and Ma moved swiftly round the table to poor Jennet, almost senseless now with shock and humiliation.

"It's alright sweetheart." Ma held her head. "Better out than in. Don't worry, you can't help it. There!"

The bowl had arrived and Mistress Alice sponged her face and hands and dabbed her temples with lavender oil. Smelling salts were applied and Ma helped clean up with lavender oil and spices. The covered bowl was handed to Anne. Bobbing a

84

swift curtsey to the Company at large, she whisked it away, shutting the door softly behind her. They could hear her footsteps tap-tapping away down the stone flagged hallway in the direction of the kitchen. The Chovihani regarded the proceedings with a look of sardonic amusement on her hawk-like face, but the Mistresses Chattox and Demdike sat as if turned to stone. The Silver Hare spoke as though nothing at all had happened.

"Continue, Atterlothe, if you please."

Slowly and clearly, in mild tones with no particular note of accusation, he related what Jennet had unwittingly revealed in the Smith living room. Old Demdike leapt to her feet and swore horribly at Jennet and would have struck her had she not been restrained by Figwort and Wayland Smith.

"Treacherous brat!" she shrieked in a terrible voice. "To betray your own grandmother. You think you're a lady now your precious Smiths have taken you in, but its Demdike blood flows in your veins, my girl. If I'm bad, you're tainted too, just like all the Demdikes before us. I curse you…"

"Enough!" The Silver Hare spoke in a voice colder than ice. "Do not compound your crime by bullying the innocent child who yet loves you. Keep your curses to yourself."

"It wasn't just me." Cornered, old Demdike in her rage and fear at being found out was unstoppable in her outpouring of poison. "Ask her!" She pointed a shaking finger at Mistress Chattox who sat white and slack jawed with fear. "Ask her, go on. She was in it too. Ask her about the mandrake she keeps under her bed. Ask her about the baby's skulls…"

The Silver Hare sighed and raised a paw. A shaft of rainbow light shot towards the two old women and they both became as still as the carved thrones they were seated on.

"Children of Darkness," it said sadly, "do you think I did not know of your fall from grace? The Silver Hare sees all things, past, present, future. You stepped from the path of light by your own free will. The way of the Great Mother was not enough for you. Yet you may step back again if you so choose. Your foolishness has put yourselves and others in great peril,

85

but you may yet have the chance to redeem yourselves and save them, if you can be as brave as you have been foolish. You will remain still now and listen." It inclined its silver head towards the Chovihani. "My sister, I think you wish to speak to The Company."

Aunt Salome nodded gravely. She rose to her feet and exchanged a meaningful look with Atterlothe.

"Since midsummer," she began in her deep voice, "we have not been idle. The Egyptians and the Faery Clans have spent much time together in consultation. The Way of the Great Mother must not be obliterated by foolishness." She cast a glance of disgusted scorn at old Demdike. "Therefore, we have a plan. We wish to practice The Glamour."

Mistress Alice gasped and a ripple of astonishment came from the older Smiths. The Silver Hare gave her a keen look.

"Pray continue." it said, "but first explain to us the meaning of the term."

"The Glamour is a complex spell often practiced by the Egyptians. It is the art of making objects or people seem other than they are. Even to hold the Glamour for a few minutes requires great skill and energy. What we are about to propose," here she glanced again at Atterlothe, "has never been attempted before. Our intention is to create life-size puppets in the exact image of the members of the Demdike and Chattox families and of Mistress Alice. We will use our most skilled carvers and spells from the faery clans to make them so lifelike that no mortal will know the difference. When the time comes, it will be the puppets who are arrested, the puppets who stand trial and the puppets who are imprisoned and hanged."

Pa spoke in bewilderment.

"But the puppets are animated by the puppet master who moves the strings. How can motionless puppets fool anyone? And for such a length of time."

Atterlothe rose to his feet and addressed the Company.

"It is a difficult, audacious plan. To carry it out, we intend to enlist the help of the Spirits of the Dead. They will animate the puppets as long as required."

There was a stunned silence. Emmet remembered meeting the Chovihani in the graveyard and the ancient ghosts - the three Demdike sisters. Now he understood what Aunt Salome, Figwort and Atterlothe had been doing there.

"This would indeed be a bold endeavour," said the Silver Hare. "It could work. It would mean invoking ancient magic and would not be easy. The Spirits of the Dead cannot be coerced against their will. This is an enormous thing to ask of them. Their time in the world of men is over and our world is no longer their concern. This will mean asking them to leave the eternal peace of their resting place and inhabit inanimate bodies, not even human. By the laws of Ancient Magic, to force them to do so would be to step from the path of light into Necromancy. This I cannot permit, not even to save our Company."

The Chovihani nodded.

"I am aware of this, my Lord. There are two instances in which the dead can be called upon in this way. One is through the ties of the blood, of family. The other is rarer, but stronger, and that is through the ties of love."

The Silver Hare made a tiny motion with its right paw and old Demdike and Old Chattox began to move again. They were both pale, scowling dreadfully, but neither attempted to speak.

"In order to maintain the Glamour," said the Silver Hare, "one or more of our number will have to remain with the puppets at all times. I wonder how this is to be accomplished. They will be in constant company of the Dead and their life-force in peril. Dangerous indeed. Perhaps," it paused for another moment, "fatal."

Hetty had a sudden insight and thought to herself, 'The Silver Hare knows what will happen! It knew about Old Demdike already. It knows everything. What is the point of all this when it already knows?' She glanced at her twin and knew they were of the same mind. The Silver Hare looked at them in a kindly manner.

"What is it, sisters? Do you wish to speak?"

Hetty reddened, but she spoke up bravely.

"Sir," she began, and faltered, not knowing how to voice what she wanted to say. Letty spoke for them both.

"Please, Lord, if you can see all things, past and future, then you must know the answers. Can't you just make everything right?"

"My children, if only it were that simple. Even the Silver Hare cannot change what will be. When you are older and more experienced, you will understand this better."

Lily piped up, surprising everyone. "That's not an answer." she said crossly. "Grown ups always say you'll understand better when you're older. That just means they don't want to tell you," then added darkly, "or they don't know themselves."

"Lily!" Ma was horrified. "Where are your manners? Please forgive her rudeness, my Lord."

The Silver Hare threw back its head and laughed, a sound like a shower of stars.

"She was not rude," it said. "The sister has a brave heart. I only light the path of the Great Mother, sweetheart. I do not reveal what is to come. I can act as the Company's conscience, and at times as its guide. All of you have free will. Every action has a consequence, just as a tiny stone dropped into a pool forms ripples that go on and on."

The girls looked uncertain and Lilt's bottom lip stuck out mutinously, but Emmet felt he almost understood.

"You mean," he began shyly, "that we do stuff, and things happen, and it's kind of our fault even if we didn't know, then we must try to sort it out ourselves. You can point us in the right direction, but you can't make us…"

"Exactly so," the Silver Hare said approvingly. "In the end, we must follow the dictates of our hearts and our consciences."

"If we have one," Saffron, perched on the edge of the table next to Lily, muttered tartly under her breath. Figwort gave her a stern look.

Atterlothe cleared his throat and spoke again. "Then do we take it, my Lord, that our plan has your approval?"

The Silver Hare regarded him steadily.

"It is a good plan, Atterlothe. Dangerous and difficult, perhaps, but a good plan none the less. Tell us how you envisage proceeding from here."

"For the next few months, the Egyptian master carvers will work with the Faery clans to make the puppets. The troupe of Egyptians will bide with us in the Faery Realms for this period. To camp for so long at Roughlee Hall would create suspicion and danger for Mistress Alice. The Company shall meet in the graveyard on All Souls Night, All Hallows Eve. The Dead have agreed to hold counsel with us then, and it is a safe night for humans to be with them, when the natural laws are suspended."

"Very well," said the Silver Hare, inclining its head. "This meeting is at an end. We shall go out into the sunshine and celebrate Lammas, the harvest that is and the harvests that are yet to be. Mistress Demdike and Mistress Chattox, you will stay behind for a few minutes. I must have speech with you alone."

Outside in the garden, Jennet breathed great lungfuls of fresh air. Anne had thoughtfully given her a spoonful of honey and a cool glass of chamomile tea with mint leaves. Preparations for the usual big feast were underway with faery musicians gaily playing music. Hetty and Letty had an arm each protectively round her waist and Lily, Emmet and Jimmy stood close by.

"Come," said Henny Penny, from under Jimmy's arm. "There are lots of people to help and it will be half an hour at least before everything is ready. They don't need us; come over into the herb garden and have a rest; you look awful."

The group wandered into the herb garden, beautifully planted in the shape of a lover's knot and surrounded by the strong scented box hedge. There were herbs all over the garden at Roughlee, but here were Mistress Alice's medicinal herbs, her pride and joy. Jennet and the twins sat down on a stone bench and the others sat around at their feet.

"How do you feel?" Emmet asked.

"Pretty awful," Jennet said at last, "but differently awful, if you know what I mean. I feel better that Granny knows. At least I don't have to worry about that anymore. But now she hates me," and her eyes filled with tears again.

Jimmy poked her foot. "Not hate Jennet." He spoke firmly in his simple way. "Granny angry, frightened. She get over it. Still her Scarlet Flower."

"She was in the wrong," said Henny Penny. "And she got caught out. People say all sorts of horrible things they don't mean. It wasn't your fault."

"I wonder what the Silver Hare is saying to them." Lily was curious. "I expect they are in awful trouble."

"I can't believe I was sick in front of the Silver Hare!"

Jennet's white face flushed scarlet at the memory. Letty, to everyone's astonishment, began to laugh. "I'm sorry!" she giggled helplessly. "Oh, I'm sorry, but it was funny. Everyone's faces! I bet no one was ever sick in a solemn meeting of the Company of the Silver Hare before."

Jennet stared at her and then her face broke into a lopsided grin. "You're right," she said, "it was a bit funny..."

They were all laughing, great howls and gusts of wonderful, healing laughter, releasing all the tension and anxiety of the last week.

Saffron arrived, fluttering over the herb garden on her rainbow wings. "Goodness," she said in surprise, "you all sound happy. Your Ma said to come and fetch you. It's time to light the bonfire in the orchard. They are all waiting to start."

She fluttered off and the children got to their feet, still wiping away tears of mirth.

"Oh," said Jennet, with a sigh. "That's so much better. Do you know, I think I'm hungry?"

The twins and Lily scampered on ahead, Lily dragging Jimmy by the hand, Emmet and Jennet following behind.

"Jennet," said Emmet, shyly, "what your granny said about your blood being tainted, all that horrible stuff?"

"Yes?" Jennet stopped in the middle of the path. Her eyes

90

were wary.

"I just wanted to say, I think you are a good person, the best person I've ever known in all my life. I know you aren't bad. You've helped me so much in so many ways. Having you live with us is lovely. All our family love you, and Jimmy and Henny Penny. Your blood isn't tainted. I don't even know what that means, but I don't believe it, and I hope you stay with us for ever."

Jennet was silent for so long that Emmet began to feel foolish and his face grew red. Perhaps he had revealed too much of himself. Then she flung her arms around him and gave him a huge hug, so unexpected that he almost lost his balance. She buried her face in his shirt. He hugged her back gently. He could feel all her bones; it was like holding a bird. He bent his head and just for a moment did what he had longed to do ever since he had met her. He buried his face in her wild red hair and took a deep breath. It smelt exactly as he always knew it would smell, like coming home. Jennet pulled gently away. Her green eyes shone like stars in the paleness of her face.

"Thank you, Emmet," she said. "I'm so happy living with your family, too. I hope… we can stay forever."

A shadow passed across her face and Emmet opened his mouth to ask her what was wrong, but Lily came running back to them.

"Come on," she called, "it's time for the bonfire and I'm starving."

11. Gateway to the Faery Realms

The next day, the Smiths were relieved to see that Jennet and Jimmy seemed their old, happy, enthusiastic selves again. It was as though they had come though a trial and passed through it unscathed. The Lammas celebrations had been joyous and delightful as ever, and although Old Demdike had ignored her grandchildren, she had not been actively unpleasant to them either. Lily tactfully put Mistress Mary back in her box under the bed and played instead with the family of corn dollies which Ma had made for her.

The rest of the summer was a busy and happy time. All the vegetables in the garden were coming at once, and food was abundant in its variety. Ma was a skilled, thrifty housewife and was always busy in the dairy and the stillroom, brewing, salting, laying away and drying for the winter, which seemed far away to the children, but which Ma was well aware of, looming ever closer. Pa, Emmet and Jimmy were constantly going out with axes to the woods and fields around the village. The pile of logs besides the forge grew high and Emmet spent half an hour or so every morning with his axe, chopping firewood before the day grew too warm. He loved the swing and the rhythm of the axe and grew fitter from the exercise. His puppy fat fell away from him and he grew taller and leaner. Minus his spots and no longer plump, Emmet was happier and more comfortable in his own skin than he had ever been before. He also worked every day with his father in the forge. Wayland Smith was pleased with his progress.

"You've the makings of a fine smith, son," he said. "You are coming on in leaps and bounds."

"I don't know if I'll ever be as good as you, Pa," Emmet said shyly.

Pa's face clouded. "I hope for your sake you won't be son," he said soberly. "Living for ever is... well, it's a long time, that's all."

Emmet looked at his father inquisitively. They had been

so busy with the ordinary business of daily life that it was easy to forget at times that they were anything other than an ordinary family.

Jennet popped her head in and said, "Suppers almost ready. And Atterlothe's here. We'll eat inside, Ma says."

At some point since Lammas, Jennet and Jimmy had, by some tacit agreement, stopped calling them Master and Mistress Smith and begun calling them Ma and Pa. They stopped visiting Malkin Tower, the Demdike home, and never mentioned their real family at all. The Smiths knew that at some point matters would have to be addressed, but for the moment they wisely accepted the situation and allowed the matter to rest.

"Ten minutes," said Pa cheerfully. "We'll just finish off here and then we'll be in."

They damped down the furnace, put their tools away neatly and laid aside their work. Emmet fetched a bucket of water from the well and they washed the grime from their hands and faces. All were seated around the table in the cottage, tucking into Ma's famous rabbit stew.

After the meal was over and the clearing up done, Pa and Atterlothe lit their pipes.

"Is this just a social call?" said Pa after they had puffed in companionable silence for a few minutes.

"Not exactly," replied Atterlothe. "I come from the Chovihani. The carving of the puppets is under way and Jimmy and Jennet are needed by the artists to have their likenesses taken."

Ma and the girls were slicing apples into rings at the kitchen table to hang on to strings and dry for the winter. Jennet put down her knife and wiped her thin fingers on her apron. She didn't look at Atterlothe.

"Where will we have to go?" Her voice was rather strained. "To the Faery Realms?"

Atterlothe understood what was worrying her. "Your Granny won't be there. It will be only you and Jimmy. However, if your Ma and Pa can spare you, I wondered if you all might like to come."

His words had an electrifying effect. Lily leapt off her stool, knocking it over, and scattering apple rings in every direction. The twins jumped up and spun each other round in delight.

"Faeryland, Faeryland, we're all going to Faeryland!" Lily whooped at the top of her voice.

Ma spoke sternly but there was a twinkle in her eye.

"If any more apple rings are spoilt, no one shall go anywhere. Lily set that stool to rights, and Hetty and Letty pick up those rings; you are trampling all over them. Now go and wash them. That's better."

"Can you spare us Pa?" Emmet longed to go but was aware of how much work the bright September days brought with them.

"I don't see why not." Pa looked thoughtful. "It's my understanding that time runs differently in the Faery Realms, eh, Atterlothe?"

Atterlothe nodded. "This is true. Sometimes one may return from what seemed like a single day to find that years have passed in human time. The reverse is also true. We can arrange things so that no time at all will seem to have passed here until you return."

"When will we go?" Jennet asked.

"Well," Atterlothe pretended to consider, "there is no time like the present, is there?"

"Where are the Faery Realms?" asked Lily. "Is it far? Will I need my cloak? How shall we get there?"

"So many questions." Atterlothe was amused. "The Faery Realms are all around, for those who have eyes to see. However, they exist in another dimension. It is not easy to explain it to you. As for getting there, why, you shall use your keys."

"What keys?" Letty was puzzled. "We don't have any keys."

"Your amulets," said Pa. "You do still have your amulets, I suppose?"

94

Each child touched their amulet. The tiny Silver Hares had never been removed since they had been given to them.

"Good," Atterlothe rose from his seat. "All we now need is the nearest lock."

Pa led the way through the connecting door into the smithy. Ma moved swiftly around, casting her usual spells of protection. Pa lifted his winged helmet from the hook on which it always hung and placed it on his head. He strapped on the silver breastplate. Immediately, thought Emmet, in awe, he seemed taller, more majestic, his face more noble, his chest broader.

"Come forward children." Atterlothe beckoned them closer to Wayland Smith. "Behold the locks."

All round the edges of the intricately wrought silver breast plate were tiny hare shaped holes cut out of the metal.

"Place your keys into the locks," said Ma.

Jimmy stepped up first, Henny Penny under his arm, and fitted his Silver Hare into one of the shapes. The others followed suit and when the last was in position, the shield swung inwards. How was that possible? Where the centre of Pa should have been, there was an open space, a portal leading to another realm.

"Bring your keys and follow me," said Atterlothe, calmly.

Afterwards, the children found it hard to remember precisely what happened. Either the space in the centre of Wayland Smith grew larger or Atterlothe and the children grew smaller. Somehow, they found themselves drawn through the portal whilst the universe re-arranged itself just as it had when their wishes had been granted on Midsummer's Eve.

For a moment, Emmet felt giddy. The universe gently stopped moving and he found himself grasping Jennet's hand so tightly that she yelped. The others stood with him in a huddle, slightly shocked, apart from Atterlothe who wore his usual bland expression.

They stood on the edge of a green glade. It seemed that they had stepped out of a doorway cut from the air in front of them, through which they could still see the interior of the smithy with Ma giving them an airy wave before the door swung shut. Now there was nothing at all to show where it had been. Lily cautiously put her hand out to feel, but it passed through empty space. This was too much for her, and her face crumpled.

"I want Ma," she wailed loudly. "I want to go home. I don't like it here."

Emmet put his arm around her. He still felt none too good himself.

"It's alright Lily," he soothed. "Atterlothe wouldn't bring us anywhere that wasn't safe. And we can go home whenever we want to, can't we?" He glanced rather uncertainly at Atterlothe as he spoke.

Atterlothe grinned reassuringly. "Of course. You are not prisoners in the Faery Realms. This was intended as a treat, Lily. Please don't cry. Let's all sit down for a minute and have some liquid life force. That will make you feel better."

They sat on the soft moss that carpeted the green glade. Atterlothe took a small horn cup from his scrip, and the bottle of liquid life force, and gave each child a few drops. All experienced the familiar golden glow and Emmet felt himself growing calmer. Lily stopped crying.

"It's pretty here," she said.

The moss shone, studded with many beautiful flowers unlike any the children had ever seen before. The quality of the light was different too, softer and more golden. The glade seemed to be in the middle of a wood of silvery trees that rustled gently in the breeze. It was pleasantly warm and everywhere birds were singing.

"This is my home," said Atterlothe, simply. "You are welcome here, Children of The Five."

Jennet found her manners and said, "Thank you for bringing us here. It's beautiful and we are most honoured. It was just a bit sudden."

"And coming through Pa's middle was scary," chimed in Hetty. Letty nodded agreement.

"How could that happen?" she asked anxiously. "A great big hole where Pa's belly should be. Are we inside Pa now?"

"No," said Atterlothe, "there are many doors and portals to the Faery Realms. Because of his special relationship with the Gods, Wayland Smith has a foot in both worlds. His being is a gateway of a kind, but there are many others. Please don't ask me to explain it further. It's complicated and it doesn't matter. We will not return that way, if it disturbs you."

Hetty opened her mouth to ask another question but at that moment there was a loud chiming of silvery bells and through the trees came scurrying a herd of snowy white goats. They were tiny and slender with silky, curling hair, and their eyes were a bright, piercing blue. The leading goat was ridden gracefully by an elf-maiden. She sat bare back with her long legs dangling down on either side. She wore a floating garment of rainbow colours and her wild hair was a dazzling shade of sky blue with flowers and feathers woven into it. Her pointed face lit up when she saw Atterlothe.

"Papa! Mother sent me to meet you. Are these the Children of The Five?"

She slid down from the white goat which immediately began to munch the flowers. Atterlothe greeted her with a kiss on her bright forehead. "Yes, they are. Come and meet them."

He slipped an arm around her delicate shoulders and drew her towards the human children.

"My daughter," he announced proudly. "Speedwell."

The children were introduced one by one and Speedwell repeated each of their names after Atterlothe. "Emmet, Hetty, Letty, Lily, Jennet, Jimmy, Henny Penny," she giggled delightedly. "Such unusual names. Would you like to ride home on my goats? They won't mind."

Emmet looked dubiously at them.

"I think we might be too big," he said.

Speedwell reached into her pocket and pulled out a handful of sparkling dust, throwing it over the children whilst uttering a magical word. The universe sighed and turned itself inside out. When it was done, the children and the goats found

97

themselves perfectly matched. Atterlothe gave Speedwell a stern look, as if she had done this kind of thing before without permission, but she tossed her mad blue hair and pretended not to notice.

"Come and ride next to me, Lily," she laughed happily. "Tell me what it is like to be human."

Lily needed no second bidding. She and Speedwell were chattering away nineteen to the dozen. The white goats trotted through the silver trees at a smart pace, the children riding, Atterlothe striding along beside them. The trees reached out slender arms to stroke and pat them as they passed, which Emmet found slightly disconcerting, particularly as a long twiggy finger poked itself into his ear.

"It's alright," laughed Speedwell, seeing his anxious face. "They are dryads, tree spirits, and they are curious. They don't mean harm."

"That's as maybe," Henny Penny muttered, giving a sharp peck to a tree which had pulled out one of her tail feathers. Its branch shot back and the rustling of its leaves sounded like a yelp of pain. Looking more closely, the children saw delicate faces etched into the trunks, faces that watched as they passed.

The wood gave way to pastureland and they found themselves looking towards a beautiful castle, all slender turrets and glittering rooftops. Out of the main gate came galloping a milk-white mare with a silver mane and a golden star shining on her forehead. She was riderless and she made straight for them with a whinny of gladness. She slowed her pace as she drew near and high-stepped her way to Atterlothe, prancing with pleasure.

"Stella, my dearest friend!" Atterlothe buried his face for a moment in her shining mane and then asked, "May I?"

"Always," the mare replied.

Atterlothe swung himself onto her back and they trotted along beside the goats who were going full tilt now that they were so close to home.

They passed over the drawbridge and the children found themselves in a sunlit courtyard of golden stone where

98

fountains played and fruit trees grew in intricate flowerbeds. Speedwell slid down from her goat and the company followed suit. She then thanked the goats who nodded their white heads good-humouredly.

"Who lives here, Atterlothe?" asked Emmet.

"The Elven King," she told him.

Lily was impressed. "Ooh, Atterlothe, will we get to meet him? I'll curtsey, shall I? I'm good at curtseying. Is he friendly or is he lofty, like The Silver Hare?"

"Actually," said Atterlothe, "you know him rather well."

The children looked at him in puzzlement, except for Speedwell who gave a shriek of laughter.

"Papa is the Elven King! Didn't you know? Oh, that's so funny."

There was a long silence, broken at last by Lily who swept the most magnificent curtsey.

"Your Royal Highness!" she cried in ringing tones. Then in her usual voice, "That was my best one yet!"

Speedwell was almost crying with laughter. Atterlothe looked embarrassed. "Lily, you don't have to curtsey. My title bears no weight in the human world. I am still your family friend, as I always have been. Nothing is changed. Come in now and meet my wife."

He strode inside, gesturing for them to follow. Speedwell pulled herself together with a visible effort.

"Pa doesn't much like being King," she confided to them in a low tone. "He has only become one since Grandpapa died last year. He likes to wear old clothes and smoke his pipe and go off on adventures. It's a pity Figwort couldn't have been king, he would have loved it."

"Is Figwort here then?" asked Jennet.

"Yes, he's the Prime Minister. He's a good one too. He sees to all the things that Papa forgets."

Emmet digested all this new information slowly.

"That makes you a princess, then. Princess Speedwell."

To his surprise, Speedwell turned pink and her eyes filled with tears.

"Yes, I am, but please don't call me that," she begged. "I liked it when we were just ordinary. I hate dressing up and wearing a crown and having to be on my best behaviour. I hoped we were going to be friends. Please don't treat me differently."

Lily gave her a hug and a big wet kiss.

"Of course we'll be friends. Could I try your crown on though?"

"Lily!" Emmet was horrified. "What a thing to ask."

Speedwell laughed through her tears. "I don't mind. Lily, you're so funny. After supper we can play dressing up in my royal clothes, if you like."

Lily was thrilled. "I wish I had beautiful blue hair like yours."

"That's easy."

Speedwell flicked a pinch of faery dust, said a magic word and the universe shrugged its shoulders. Instantly Lily found herself sporting a wild mane of blue hair.

"Thank you! I love it here!"

Hetty and Letty were enchanted.

"Pink, please!"

"Purple?"

It was a colourful group that was taken in to meet the Elven Queen.

"This is my beloved wife, Savine." Atterlothe kissed her hand reverently and led her forward. "Meet the Children of The Five, my dear."

Savine was a tall and elegant elf-woman, an older version of Speedwell with the same bright blue eyes and pointed face, although her hair was silvery, like moonbeams, worn in a long braid over one shoulder which hung almost to the floor. She was dressed in a plain green gown with a narrow circlet of gold on her beautifully shaped head. Her eyes twinkled in amusement as they rested on the girls.

"You are all welcome, Children of The Five." Her voice was husky and made them think of warm thick honey. "I can see you have already made friends with Speedwell."

100

Lily beamed at her. "After supper we are going to play dressing up and she's going to let me wear her crown."

Atterlothe and Savine exchanged amused glances.

"Then we should have supper so that you can start. Come through and be seated. You must all be hungry after your journey."

She led them through a graceful archway into a wonderful room hung with silken tapestries and velvet covered couches, although it had no roof and was open to the sky and gardens beyond.

"What happens if it rains?" asked Jennet.

"It gets diverted," was the somewhat enigmatic reply.

A table was laid in the centre of the room with a simple meal of bread and honey, cheese and many delicious smelling fruits which the children had never seen before. A dark figure rose from a divan and moved towards them. The children recognised the hawk-like face and gold earrings of the Chovihani.

"Well met, Children of The Five." Her voice was as sardonic as ever. "We meet in many different places, no?"

The girls bobbed curtsies and Emmet gave his usual awkward bow. It occurred to him that they had not done this for the Elvish Queen and he wondered what it was about the Chovihani which made them fearful of causing her offence. Savine seemed to feel no such awkwardness. She slipped her arm into that of the tall Egyptian and drew her towards the table.

"At last they are here, Aunt Salome, and we can eat. It is so lovely to have you staying with us. I do enjoy our chats together. I must ask your advice on the new charm I am working on."

They might have left the smithy just after supper, but they were now hungry all over again. Maybe this was one effect of travel into the realm of Faery.

"It must be the middle of the night at home," Emmet thought. "Time is certainly different here."

Atterlothe invoked the Blessing of the Great Mother and

101

the company fell to with a will.

"You will find no meat in the Faery Realms," Savine told them gently. "I understand from Atterlothe that in the human world, where people do not understand the speech of animals, birds and beasts are freely eaten, but here, we do not think it right to eat our brothers and sisters."

Henny Penny nodded her feathered head in vigorous agreement.

"But," thought Lily unhappily, "if we stopped eating meat, that would mean no more of Ma's rabbit pie."

They tucked in to the delicious food and only stopped when Speedwell said, "Come on Lily, Hetty and Letty." She jumped up from the table. "Haven't you finished yet? Do let's go and play. I have so much to show you."

"Sweetheart," Savine was gently reproving, "what should you say to us?"

Speedwell sighed impatiently but curtsied obediently and intoned politely enough, "Thank you for a lovely supper, Mother, Papa, Aunt Salome. May we be excused?"

Atterlothe's mouth twitched suspiciously but Savine remained sweetly serious.

"Certainly, my dears. Have a lovely time."

Lily abandoned the moral dilemma of the rabbit pie and scampered after the others who were already halfway out of the door. Atterlothe gave a rueful laugh. "I fear we shall be hard put to make a princess of our daughter."

"She has much spirit," commented the Chovihani, "and that is not a bad thing in a princess. She is young, she will learn. Time tempers many things." She turned abruptly to Jennet. "And you child, how much spirit do you have?"

Jennet was taken aback by the question and turned bright red. "I don't know," she stammered.

"More than you think, my girl, more than you think." The Chovihani eyed her thoughtfully. "And you will need it, child, oh yes, you will need it."

This last she seemed to say almost to herself and Jennet caught Emmet's eye with a troubled glance. Aunt Salome

gazed into the distance for a few moments, deep in thought, but recollected herself.

"You have come here for a purpose, no? Not just to have your hair turned all colours of the rainbow. It is time to come and meet the master carvers. Your Royal Highnesses?"

Atterlothe gave a grimace.

"No need to stand on ceremony, Aunt Salome. We are alone after all. Yes of course. I shall accompany you, if I may. Their skill fascinates me."

They all rose from the table.

"Forgive me if I remain here," said Savine. "I have things to attend to and I would like to remain on hand for the little ones in case Speedwell gets carried away."

Atterlothe pressed her hand affectionately and led the others out of the lovely outdoor room to the gardens beyond. The children gazed around them as they walked. Wherever they cast their eyes there were new wonders, more delights. Everything seemed sharper, brighter, more graceful and colourful than the world they were accustomed to at home. Indeed, home seemed far away, a distant memory.

Atterlothe beckoned them through a golden gate into an orchard of trees bearing the most beautiful amber-coloured apples that Emmet had ever seen. The scent of them was overpowering and they seemed to glow with an inner light. Here, amongst the trees, the Egyptians had made their camp, the familiar benders with their gaudy decorations forming a rough circle as much as the trees permitted.

The scent of the wood smoke drifted towards them from a small cooking fire. An old woman stirred an iron pot and a group of men sat smoking on a fallen log. Children tumbled and played with a number of small faeries, and some women with dark curls were washing clothes in a wooden tub, hanging them in the trees to dry. Beneath a striped awning on two carved chairs sat Mistress Alice and Old Chattox. The party advanced towards them, Jennet hanging back, slightly anxious at having to meet her grandmother's old crony. Emmet and Jimmy bowed politely, and Jennet bobbed a curtsey.

Atterlothe laughed delightedly.

"Excellent," he said. "They are perfect in every way."

Emmet gave him a puzzled look. "Good evening Mistress Alice, Mistress Chattox," he said shyly. "Have you come to have your likenesses taken as well?"

There was no answer from the two women. They remained motionless, staring straight ahead. A short Egyptian with a good-humoured face detached himself from the group of smokers and bowed in the rather mocking way the gypsies had.

"So," he grinned, "the ladies, they don't answer, no?"

Light dawned on Jimmy's face. He went right up to Mistress Alice and, to the bewilderment of Jennet and Emmet, touched her nose, then turned to the company, beamed and said, "Not real. Puppets."

Emmet's jaw dropped.

"But they are so…"

"Lifelike. Yes, I know. The skill of the master carvers is quite astonishing. Obadiah, you have done a remarkable job."

"Thank you, your Highness. Are these two young uns the next to be done?"

"They are," said Atterlothe.

Obadiah walked around Jimmy and Jennet one way and then back the other. He lifted a strand of Jennet's wild red hair and making a frame of his fore fingers and thumbs, peered through it at Jimmy.

"We must allow for growth," he muttered to himself. "They are children, and children grow. But how much will they grow over the winter? That's the question."

He dragged a couple of stools from the nearest bender and gestured to Jennet and Jimmy to sit on them.

"Markus," he called. "Bring charcoal and parchment. Stop lazing on that log. There is much work to be done."

"Come Emmet," Atterlothe put an arm across his shoulders. "We shall only be in the way now. Let us leave them to it. Aunt Salome, are you coming with us?"

The Chovihani shook her head. "I have business here with

my people. We shall meet later."

12. The Choosing

"What would you like to see?" Atterlothe asked Emmet, as they strolled through the gardens. "We have some time on our hands now. We could go and feed the dragons, if you wish. Or I believe a pod of mermaids are visiting in the bay." He looked at Emmet thoughtfully. "Perhaps not the mermaids this time. They can never resist a handsome young male human. You are just the right age and they will try to lure you away. No, I have it, we shall visit Stella and her new foal."

He strode away purposefully with Emmet struggling to keep up, his head spinning. Dragons! Mermaids!

Emmet had never seen the sea. He didn't think he wanted to be lured away from Jennet. And Atterlothe said he was handsome. Surely that couldn't be true, could it?

They rounded a corner and found themselves in an open meadow surrounded by mighty oak trees with the wizened faces of gnarled old men. Atterlothe gave a musical whistle and the same beautiful white mare trotted toward them out of the wood. She nuzzled Atterlothe's shoulder with her soft nose.

"My Liege," she said, warmly.

"Stella," Atterlothe drew Emmet forward, "I have brought this young man to meet you properly. He is Emmet, son of Wayland Smith."

The white mare's intelligent eyes flickered with interest.

"Our dear Wayland. He shod me with my diamond shoes. Such a wonderful smith and a human of great integrity. So, you are his child. I am delighted to make your acquaintance."

Emmet half bowed, unsure if bowing to a horse was the correct etiquette in Faeryland. He was saved by Stella herself.

"If you wish, you may caress my nose," she murmured.

Emmet loved horses and had shod many whilst helping at home in the forge. Reaching out, he stroked her velvety face and scratched behind her snowy white ears. She gave a snort of pleasure.

"He has the touch, just like his father. A little to the left if you please. Mmm, that's it."

"Where is your child, Stella? We came to see how she was getting on. Why, she's right here."

Atterlothe gazed fondly on a tiny, long legged foal, just stepping out from behind her mother.

"She is never far from me," said Stella. "I left her briefly with the Dryads when I came to meet you earlier, but she wasn't happy. You know what new babies are - they only want their mother."

The foal stepped towards them. It was exactly like Stella, a miniature version, with the same golden star on its white forehead. Emmet looked into its dark blue eyes and his heart turned over. The foal moved towards him. Emmet found himself on his knees and the creature bent and pressed its golden star against his forehead. An extraordinary sensation came over him, as though the golden star was fusing to his head, golden light flowing into his heart and veins. He could feel what it was like to be the foal. Indeed, he didn't know where he began and the foal ended. It was as though they had joined together and become one entity.

Slowly the foal drew back and Emmet rose to his feet. They were no longer touching yet Emmet knew they were still joined. He became aware of Stella and Atterlothe gazing at them with something approaching awe. There was a long silence, broken at last by Atterlothe.

"She has Chosen," he said, astonished. "I have never seen it happen in a foal so young."

"And she has Chosen a human. How can that be? I did not know that such a thing was possible."

Stella tossed her white head and the sunlight caught the gold of the star making a dancing pattern on the leather of Atterlothe's boots.

"And yet the Choosing is never wrong. Emmet, my child does you a great honour. You, and only you, will be her lifelong companion and rider. She has Chosen. This is a bond that can be broken only by death."

Emmet sensed that he ought to be surprised, but he wasn't. He felt serene and calm and complete.

"Now you have been chosen, Emmet, you must name her," Atterlothe said, gravely. "This is the tradition between Faery horse and rider. Think carefully, for this name will shape your lives together. Take your time, as much as you need, for we may not help you. It is something only you can do."

But Emmet already knew her name.

"She is called Pooka." He spoke with quiet assurance.

Stella and Atterlothe exchanged glances.

"That is a good name," said Atterlothe, quietly. "It means Spirit Horse whose task is to carry dead heroes to paradise. The path you ride together will be an interesting one."

"Pooka," Stella sighed.

The foal pricked up her long white ears as though she already knew her name, and then nuzzled at her mother for milk. Atterlothe laughed heartily. "It will be a while before she is big enough to carry a hero, living or dead."

"Did you choose Atterlothe?" Emmet asked Stella, shyly.

"Yes Emmet, I did. More years past than I care to remember now. Five hundred and thirty I believe."

"Five hundred and thirty-one, I think you'll find," said Atterlothe thoughtfully.."

Emmet was staggered. "How old are you, Atterlothe?"

"Five hundred and forty-two next birthday. Quite young to be Elven King, I know, but I've always been level-headed."

Pooka had finished feeding and nudged her nose into Emmet's palm. He knelt and put his arm around her neck. "Thank you for choosing me," he whispered.

"She doesn't talk yet," Stella licked her foal fondly. "She was only born yesterday. But she will learn. And she will always remember you. I do not know how or when you two will be together as horse and rider, for you come from different worlds, but the Choosing is never wrong and when it is your time, you will find a way. Have no fear."

They stayed a while in the meadow, Atterlothe and Stella chatting together of this and that with the old oak Dryads

throwing in the odd comment in slow, rumbling voices. Emmet stayed kneeling by the foal who folded her legs under her and snuggled up to him. He stroked her nose and plaited daisies into her mane, talking to her as he had never talked to anyone before about Ma and Pa, about his sisters, about Jimmy and Jennet, his hopes and his fears and his dreams. Pooka listened and licked his hand from time to time, the late sunlight catching the gold of her star and making it sparkle. For the first time in his life, Emmet felt he had found someone who completely understood him. He felt contented, happy and drowsy. His voice tailed off and he rested his head on Pooka's neck. He must have slept, for he was aroused by Atterlothe gently shaking his shoulder.

"Come Emmet, it is time to go. The master Carvers will have finished for tonight. The light is fading fast."

Emmet sat up with a start. The sun was dipping over the horizon and he felt a chill breeze on his face after the warmth of Pooka's body. He looked up at Atterlothe.

"How can I leave her?"

"You will leave her because you must. She is only a baby and she needs her mother. I understand how you feel Emmet. She is a part of you now, even as Stella is a part of me. She has to grow up, and so do you. She is safe here in the Faery Realms and you will visit her often."

As though she understood, the foal rose awkwardly to her feet and pressed her star to Emmet's forehead. Immediately, he felt flooded with warmth and reassurance. He kissed her nose and stood up.

"She says it's all right." He patted her one last time. "She knows I have to go, for now, and she will be waiting for me to return. I'm ready, Atterlothe."

Atterlothe gripped his shoulder and the two made their goodbyes to Stella and the dryads, slowly wending their way back to the orchard.

It was almost dark by the time they reached the lamp lit benders. Jennet and Jimmy looked glazed and exhausted, and a plump Egyptian woman was berating Obadiah the Master

Carver soundly.

"You've worn out these poor children. Look at them, they can't sit like statues for hours and hours without a break. Let them go and rest now, there is always tomorrow. Besides the light is gone. How can you see? Stop this foolishness and come and have your supper."

She broke off when she saw Emmet and the Elven King strolling towards them through the trees.

"You are right, Naomi," said Atterlothe gravely. "All things should stop for a good supper. Obadiah, rest now. You have made an excellent start. I must take these children to their beds. We will return tomorrow bright and early. I thank you for your dedicated hard work."

The old man nodded reluctantly, an artist torn from his work against his will. He slowly began to put his tools together. He had strung several lanterns in the tree above his head to try to combat the gathering dusk, and in their light Emmet gazed awestruck at the wooden heads he and Markus had begun to carve. Even though they were still in their early stages, the likenesses to Jimmy and Jennet were extraordinary.

"Early then," said Obadiah, still grumpy at being forced to stop before he was ready. "There is still much to be done."

"We shall be up with the lark," promised Atterlothe.

"Come Jimmy and Jennet. I think bed is calling."

They walked home through the gardens. It was completely dark except for two golden beams of star-shaped light which seemed to shine on the path ahead of them. Jennet looked around in puzzlement, trying to see where the light was coming from. She stopped and gave a gasp of astonishment.

"Emmet, your forehead, it's shining! You've got a star on it!"

Emmet put a hand to his forehead.

"Have I, truly?"

"Yes, you have. So has Atterlothe. What does it mean?"

"It means," Atterlothe said mildly, "that Emmet is one of the Chosen."

Emmet tried to explain to Jennet and Jimmy about his

110

experience in the meadow with Atterlothe helping him whenever he faltered.

Jennet didn't seem pleased.

"Yes, but what does it mean?" she demanded, almost rudely. Emmet looked at her in surprise. Atterlothe glanced at her and his eyes crinkled in amusement.

"It means," he said, "that Emmet will have to wear his hair long and get used to wearing a hat when he is at home in the world of men."

Jennet glared at Atterlothe and sniffed, loudly.

By now, the lights of the castle shone out a bright welcome to them, hiding the faint shining of the stars.

"Come in," said Atterlothe to the children. He tried to take Jennet's arm but she twisted away from him with a pettish gesture and stalked in by herself.

"What's wrong with her?" Emmet was worried and hurt. He wanted Jennet to be pleased for him.

"Emmet, Emmet," said Attherlothe, "the ways of women are hard to fathom."

Henny Penny piped up sharply from under Jimmy's arm. "Don't tease him, Atterlothe. She's jealous, young Emmet, that's what's wrong."

Emmet looked from one to the other of them in bewilderment.

"Jealous?" he echoed. "Jealous of what?"

Jimmy took pity on him.

"Jennet jealous of Pooka," he explained patiently. "Not want to share her Emmet with another girl," he grinned, "even if other girl is horse."

Atterlothe, Henny Penny and Jimmy exploded with laughter.

"Oh, Emmet," Atterlothe sighed, wiping his eyes, "you have so much to learn. And I shall so enjoy watching you do it."

The outdoor room was magical with lanterns and candles. Savine and the girls were seated comfortably on the cushion-strewn couches with drinks and trays of sweet meats on a low table beside them. A fire burned in a bowl before them, giving off a welcome glow with many colours dancing in the flames. The Elven Queen was telling stories and, as she did so, her graceful hands created moving pictures in the air. Lily sat on her lap with her thumb in her mouth whilst Hetty and Letty sat snuggled one on each side of Speedwell. They were spellbound with delight and made a pretty tableau in the soft illumination.

Jennet had seated herself next to Savine and her huge green eyes were fixed on her animated face, but she wore a familiar wooden expression. Emmet knew that she wasn't listening to the stories. Savine lifted Lily gently from her lap as the others came in and stood up for Atterlothe's kiss. The story-pictures faded from the air and the girls stirred and stretched as the spell was broken.

"Jimmy," Lily rushed up and hugged him, "we've had such a lovely time. Do you like my wings?"

She was sporting a costume of gorgeous garments and fabrics put together with a splendid disregard for style or colour co-ordination. Rainbow wings were growing from her small shoulders and the entire ensemble was topped by a large jewel-bedecked crown which had slipped down over one eye and hung at a rakish angle.

Hetty and Letty were similarly attired, perhaps showing slightly more sartorial restraint. Speedwell looked at them and beamed at her.

"They do look wonderful, don't they?" she said. "Show Papa how you can fly, Lily."

Lily's small face assumed a look of fierce concentration. The rainbow wings flapped stiffly and she rose into the air, Savine hastily pushing her away from the fire as she did so.

"Wonderful, Lily," said Atterlothe. "I am impressed."

Lily beamed at him proudly and circled the room with some difficulty, knocking over a bowl of fruit and candelabra as she did so.

"A little higher perhaps, sweetheart," suggested the ever-patient Elven Queen, tossing a shower of faery dust that picked

112

up the fruit and steadied the candelabra.

Lily alighted on another sofa, stood up, and curtsied deeply.

"Beautifully done," Atterlothe and the audience gave the girl a round of applause. "But now," he said, as the clapping died away, "I think we should retire for the night. It has been a busy day and we must be up early in the morning or Obadiah will wish to know the reason why. There are rooms prepared for you all and I think you will find everything that you need."

"Could Hetty, Letty and Lily sleep in my room?" begged Speedwell. "Oh ple-e-ease!"

"Of course," said Savine, "but you must settle down straight away and sleep. No more playing. Tomorrow is another day."

Atterlothe kissed Speedwell tenderly. "Goodnight, beautiful girl. Good night, Hetty, Letty and Lily. Off you go."

The children skipped out of the room, chattering as they went.

"Jimmy and Emmet," said Atterlothe, "come with me."

He led them away, Henny Penny tucked, as always, under Jimmy's arm. Jennet was left on the couch beside Savine. The wooden expression had left her face, but she looked pinched and unhappy. The Elven Queen was sympathetic.

"Would it help to tell me about it?" she suggested, softly.

Jennet's green eyes filled with tears. "It's Emmet," she said. "He's been... Chosen... and... and..." Her voice tailed away helplessly. She didn't know how to put her feelings into words. Savine took her hand. "I understand," she said, slowly. "Stella has a new foal and I saw the star upon Emmet's brow when he came in. Now you are afraid that this Choosing will take Emmet's love away from you. This is so, is it not?" Jennet gave her a startled look and turned red. Savine went on, "Emmet is your own True Love and will be until the day he dies. You do not need to fear on that score."

Jennet stared at her, astonished. "How do you know?"

Savine sighed. "True Love is rare. There is a special aura around those who have it. You and Emmet are unusual in that you are so young, but that makes it all the more powerful, just as Pooka is young to make her Choosing. There are powerful forces at play here. Let me tell you a story. Many years ago, in the morning of the world, when Atterlothe and I were young lovers, he too was Chosen and I was so jealous I thought my heart would break."

Jennet was wide-eyed. "What did you do?"

"I went to see Stella, to beg her to leave my love alone, to Choose someone else. Stella was kind. She explained the enormous honour of the Choosing, how she had no control over it, how it comes from a higher power, from the Great Mother Herself and that it should make Atterlothe even greater and more important in my eyes. She also told me that the love between horse and rider is different from the love between a man and a woman, and that I should never feel afraid. Since then, I never have."

Jennet was silent for a few moments. "Savine?" she asked, hesitantly.

"Yes, sweetheart?"

"Do you think Emmet knows that he is my own True Love?"

"My child, men are often slow about these things. Often, we women have to be patient whilst we wait for them to catch up. Also, Emmet is not yet a man, just as you are not yet a woman, but I believe in his heart, yes, he knows it."

Jennet sighed. "I was horrid to him," she said honestly. "And I was rude to Atterlothe. Will they forgive me?"

"There is nothing to forgive." Atterlothe had slipped in silently. "But if you want to make Emmet happy, ask him to take you to meet Pooka tomorrow. He would love to introduce you."

"I will," said Jennet, humbly. "And I am sorry, Atterlothe, I didn't properly understand." She felt overwhelmed with tiredness. "I would like to sleep now, please."

13. TIME TO GO HOME

The children stayed for seven days in the Faery Realms. Jennet met Pooka, the carvings were finished and the girls played to their heart's content, but one bright morning, as they broke their fast in the outdoor room, Atterlothe announced that it was time to return home.

"Home?" asked Lily. "But we are at home, aren't we?"

"Proof that it is definitely time to return," said Atterlothe.

Savine rose and fetched a familiar bottle.

"Some liquid Life Force is called for, I believe."

She poured each child a dose and they drank it obediently. Emmet looked up from his empty glass, stricken.

"Ma and Pa," he said guiltily, "how could we have forgotten them? It's the busiest time, what with getting the winter wood in. What will Pa say?"

The girls looked equally guilty and bewildered.

"I want my Ma," Lily was tearful. "She won't have forgotten <u>me</u>, will she?"

"It's alright," said Savine, soothingly. "Time is different in the Faery Realms. Truly, you have been gone for no time at all. It is hard for humans to remember their lives in their own world whilst they are here. That is one reason why they shouldn't come too often or stay too long."

Speedwell burst into loud and noisy tears.

"I don't want them to go, Papa! What will I do without Hetty and Letty and Lily? Don't make them go home. Mother, can't we adopt them?"

Savine put her arms around her daughter and stroked her forehead.

"They have their own father and mother who love them very much and would miss them dreadfully. You will see them again, I promise. Don't upset yourself so."

Lily gave Speedwell one of her big wet kisses.

"Don't cry Speedwell. You are my bestest friend in all the world... next to Jimmy," she added honestly. "But Ma and Pa need us. Perhaps you could come and visit us next time. It's not as much fun as here though."

Atterlothe stood up, purposefully.

"All things are possible. Are you all ready?"

The children looked around uncertainly at each other and then nodded. Jennet went over to the Elven Queen and hugged her.

"Thank you Savine, for giving us such a lovely time and being so kind. We shall never forget our visit here."

Savine laid her soft cheek against Jennet's for a moment.

"Child of my heart," she whispered softly. "We are the True Loves of the Chosen. Never doubt it."

They clung together briefly, then Savine disengaged herself gently. "It is time."

She lifted from her head the circlet of gold and held it up so that the morning sunlight made it wink and sparkle. Emmet noticed all around the circumference an engraved pattern of tiny hares chasing each other, nose to tail.

"Do you have your keys?"

Each child took their tiny Silver Hares from around their necks and silently fitted them into place. Instantly, the Universe performed a complicated manoeuvre and the children found themselves deposited unceremoniously on the floor of the smithy. The circlet hung in the air for a moment and Speedwell's mournful face could be seen looking at them wistfully before it faded from sight.

Ma and Pa stood exactly where they had left them.

"That was a quick visit," Pa grinned cheerfully. The grin broadened as he took in Lily's appearance.

"Well, well, you appear to have gone native."

Ma was not amused. "Lily, what on earth have you done to yourself? What ever can Atterlothe have been thinking? Blue hair? Hetty and Letty, you look almost as bad. Well, I'm not having you go about like… "

"Faeries?" suggested Saffron, helpfully, perched on the mantle shelf.

Ma gave her an unfriendly look, pointed a disapproving

116

finger at her daughters and uttered a short charm. Instantly the extravagant finery disappeared, and the girls found themselves dressed in their old clothes, minus wings and with hair a normal colour.

"Oh Ma," Lily was devastated. "Couldn't we have just kept our wings?"

"Lily," said Pa gently. "You understand why that isn't possible, don't you?"

"I do, but I did love having them. Flying is fabulous! It's good to be home, although I don't suppose you missed me because you think I only just went, but now I've remembered you, well, I love you so much Ma and Pa."

She buried her face in Ma's apron and gave her a big hug. Ma hugged her back.

"We love you too, Lily, all of you."

Her bright gaze encompassed Jimmy and Jennet as well as the Smith children.

"Now, there is just time to finish the apple rings before bed."

It took a few days for life to settle down in the Smithy. The children had forgotten what it was like to work for their living, life in Atterlothe's castle being filled with ease and luxury and charms. Ma constantly had to reprimand them for tasks forgotten or left half done. Emmet told his parents, hesitantly, about Pooka and the Choosing. They listened intently and exchanged glances as the story unfolded.

"I know about the Choosing," said Pa when Emmet had finished. "I was brought into the Faery Realm to make Stella her first shoes when she came of age. Your Pooka is her child. This has many strange and interesting implications, Emmet, more than Atterlothe has revealed to you. I am not sure if you understand quite how exceptional this is. I believe, in fact, that it's the first time such an honour has been conferred on one not of the Faery race."

"That's what Atterlothe said, Pa," said Emmet. He unconsciously fingered the golden star on his brow. Away from the Faery Realms, its brightness was barely discernible, particularly in daylight, but it was still visible to the sharp eyed when he stood in shadow.

"Keep it hidden son." Ma looked anxious. "Come here." She took out her scissors, swept Emmet's hair over his forehead and deftly snipped a ragged fringe to conceal the star. "Wear a hat when you go out. No one from the village must see this."

"Atterlothe said that, too." He looked at Pa and there was a hunger in his eyes. "When will I be able to see her again? She will be growing everyday. I miss her, Pa."

Pa laid a huge hand on his son's shoulder and gave it a sympathetic squeeze.

"I don't know Emmet. Trust Atterlothe, that's all I can say for now. And carry on growing up." He looked at Emmet appraisingly. "You are well on the way." And with that, for the time being, Emmet was forced to be content.

September passed in a haze of bright sunshine and hard work. Jams, jellies, pickles and syrups were made, seeds collected, sorted, labelled and laid away carefully. The equinox was celebrated at Roughlee Hall in the usual way, but was more subdued than previous gatherings, and although the Silver Hare graced them with its presence, no meeting of The Five was called and the Egyptians were, apart from Aunt Salome, conspicuous by their absence.

Atterlothe, although cheerful, was distracted. Emmet, plucking up the courage to ask when he might see Pooka again, only received the vague and unsatisfying answer, "Soon." This left him disappointed and told him nothing at all.

October brought with it chilly mornings wrapped in ragged mists, droplets of them left in numerous spiders' webs and the leaves turned orange, russet and red, blown by a cold wind into deep drifts. Emmet and Jimmy strung conkers and the girls made scarlet necklaces from hips and haws. All were aware that they were marking time until Halloween.

With the full moon came a change in the weather. It became mild and damp and many of the old people in the village suffered badly from the rheumatics.

Jennet, Lily and the twins woke on the morning of October 31st to the sound of a steady downpour. Jennet got out of bed and padded to the window. She opened the casement and peered out into the rain.

"Ooh, shut the window, do." Saffron was snuggled on her mattress of wool, to which Lily had added a tiny blanket. "The rain is coming in. Look, my bed is getting wet."

Jennet jumped back into her warm feather bed and cuddled down, shivering.

"It's a horrible day," she said. "It won't be nice in the churchyard tonight. I wish we didn't have to go."

"I want to go." Lily was decided. "I want to see Rosie and all the others. I don't care if it rains."

The morning passed slowly. Ma was in a great good humour which even the torrential rain could not diminish. She sang blithely around the cottage as she made a rabbit pie for later.

"It's because she is going to see our brother and sisters," said Lily, wisely. "It's put her in a good mood. When I spilt the milk at breakfast, Ma didn't even slap me."

By midday, the rain had turned into a light drizzle and by the middle of the afternoon it had stopped altogether and a watery sun was shining.

"It will be a fine evening," said Pa with satisfaction, coming out of the forge in his leather apron and squinting up at the sky. "We'll work a couple of hours lads and then we'll call it a day. Early supper tonight before we set off."

Jennet and the girls were sitting by the fire making lace with Ma, whiling away the time before supper. Jennet's stomach had butterflies in it at the thought of seeing her Grandmother again, although not as badly as last time. Ma looked up from her work and asked kindly, "Are you worried, Jennet? There is no need to be."

"A little," said Jennet, "but quite excited, too."

"It will be wonderful shape shifting again." Lily was enthusiastic. "I love being a hare."

14. THE AURA OF TRUE LOVE

It was different in the graveyard when they arrived that night, compared to their summer visit. Will o'the Wisps posted all around the stonewall and perched on the gravestones gave out an eerie, bluish light. The dead seemed in a festive mood. Efforts had clearly been made to titivate their grave clothes and the sound of ghostly music echoed through the darkness. Some of the livelier spirits were dancing a jig. The deceased Smith children came hurrying up and wound their wasted arms around Mistress Smith. Rosie kissed her mother, light as the brushing of moth wings. "We are so glad to see you. Lily, come and dance with us."

Some of the Faery Clans began to arrive and the silvery light became brighter. There was an air of expectancy, as though someone had yet to arrive, pivotal to the evening's proceedings. The Chovihani loomed silently out of the shadows, the troupe of Egyptians behind her.

"Henny Penny," she said, unsmiling, "it is time."

Jimmy put Henny Penny on the ground. She gave a cluck and laid an egg. It glowed by the light of the Will o'the Wisps in rainbow colours and the familiar humming began. The Dead stopped their music and dancing, standing in a semi-circle shoulder to shoulder with the Faery Clans and the Egyptians, watching the egg. In its rainbow depths, the flickering shape grew clearer. At last, there came a loud 'crack!' and then silence as the Silver Hare emerged from the fragments, grew to its full size and regarded the gathering with its luminous eyes.

"All Souls Night," it said in its starry voice, "All Hallows Eve and all is well. The Company of the Silver Hare thanks the Dead for their hospitality this night of all nights and bids all welcome."

A ripple of pride and pleasure passed through the Faery Clans and the Spirits of the Dead, like reeds blown in the wind, at the Silver Hare's acknowledgements. There was a rushing

120

of wings overhead and six ravens alighted on some of the gravestones, transforming into the Chattox and Demdike families. Mistress Alice appeared with Figwort and Atterlothe and curtsied deeply to The Silver Hare.

"All are now present," said the Hare. "It is time to hold our counsel. Are the Old Ones awake?"

A derisive cackle came from the overgrown part of the graveyard. All heads turned as the twisted wraiths of the three Demdike sisters emerged from the undergrowth, bringing with them the strange atmosphere the children remembered from their last visit, not quite a smell, not quite a feeling. It made Hetty and Letty shiver and reach for each other's hands. It felt bitterly cold in the graveyard and Lily's teeth began to chatter.

The ancient crones approached the Company slowly and stopped within about three feet of the Silver Hare. They did not curtsey. The oldest one spoke in a hoarse voice.

"The Living want something only the Dead can deliver. We hear you, Silver Hare, and we wake this night of nights, but you must convince us before we commit ourselves. This long sleep of ours was hard won. We do not care to have it disturbed."

The Silver Hare inclined its head to her.

"We do not come to beg. That is not the way of The Company of the Silver Hare. We come to lay our cause before you and you must consider it carefully. Your own kinswomen and children are in danger. It may be that you can save them. The Silver Hare does not force or coerce. We do not deal in necromancy."

The three ancient ones nodded slowly.

"Unfold your plans to us, O Silver Hare, and we will decide for ourselves."

"First," said the Silver Hare, "the living amongst us are cold." It raised its paw, the universe turned itself inside out and when Emmet's head stopped spinning, he gazed in astonishment to find that they seemed no longer to be in the freezing graveyard but in a beautiful silken tent with a small fire and soft cushions all around one side. The other side was

121

grey and misty and cooler, in deference to the Spirits of the Dead. Atterlothe took out his familiar bottle and handed round sips to all the living. Lily's teeth stopped chattering and the twins let go of each other's hands. When all was settled, The Silver Hare began to speak.

"Our Company met last at Lammas Tide and certain knowledge was laid before us of an unwelcome nature. As a consequence, certain daring plans were put forward. I am aware that the Chovihani has spoken with the Old Ones already about this matter. Preparations have been made and the puppets have been created by the Egyptian Master Carvers with spells and magic from the Faery Clans. All is in readiness. We ask, humbly and with great deference, if any of you among the Spirits of the Dead are prepared to animate the puppets and save our Company from imprisonment and death. We do not beseech, we do not implore, nor do we barter. We have nothing to offer in return but to honour your memory. The Silver Hare has spoken."

The Hare bowed its silver head and for a moment there was silence. The youngest Demdike sister spoke.

"How many?"

Atterlothe answered. "Nine in all. Old Demdike, Mistress Demdike, Alison, Jennet and Jimmy, old Mistress Chattox, Elizabeth and Anne Chattox and Mistress Alice Nutter. Are there, among the Spirits of the Dead, nine of you who could serve our cause, who would leave the peace of your graveyard and enter again into the affairs of the world? It is no small thing we ask."

There was a rustle among the Dead, soft and uneasy, like a breeze skirling dead leaves. Old Mrs. Law, a deathly baby in each of her tattered arms, spoke up. "I bin 'ere a year now, I like it 'ere – it's easier than being outside in the world tryin' ter scratch a livin'. But it ain't right a body should be forced 'ere afore their time, not at all it ain't. I don't like that magistrate feller, Roger Nowell 'e calls himself. I'd like to pull one across 'im. 'E'd 'ave turned me out of my cottage if I'ant of died first. An'er…" She bowed her head awkwardly and shyly at Mistress Alice. "I'd do anything for 'er. She's an angel an' I don't care 'oo hears me say it. She 'elped me an' nursed me through my cholera with never a care for she might take sick 'erself. T'weren't 'er fault I breathed me last. I'll – what was that word? Hanimate? I'll hanimate her puppet for 'er. S'not like they can kill us, is it?" She went off into a guffaw of wheezy laughter, joined in by the other spirits.

Mistress Alice's eyes filled with tears and she reached out and touched Mrs. Law's bony skull. "Thank you my dear," she whispered softly.

It was Emmet's friend Billy who stepped up next, much to everyone's surprise. "Please," he said nervously. "I'm not brave, but I'd like to help Jimmy. I know folks say he's moonstruck and the like, but he was a good friend to me. He gave my Ma Henny Penny's eggs when we was starving. He helped me pull wood home that was too heavy for me, to stop Pa beating me and he tried to pull me out of Pendle Water. You'll have to show me what to do because I'm not clever, but I'll help if I can."

Jimmy gave him a big grin. "Kind Billy!" he said.

It seemed that many of the spirits were not only willing but actively keen to help. Perhaps life in the graveyard was not exciting for them. Two rather giggly and flighty young women said they would stand in for Elizabeth and Anne Chattox, and a disreputable crone said she would play the part of old Mistress Chattox. The Old Ones exchanged glances. "We wish to see the puppets," announced the oldest one.

Atterlothe threw a pinch of faery dust and uttered a strange word. There was a flash of light, the universe shuddered and there, seated in a row, were the nine puppets. Emmet gasped. They were unbelievably real. There were exclamations of astonishment from dead and living alike as they looked from each puppet to its human counterpart and back again.

"Well," said old Mrs. Law, "tis a wondrous thing and no mistake."

"It will work," Atterlothe spoke with assurance. "With the

, The Company of the Silver Hare

help of the Spirits of the Dead, I do not see how it can fail."

The Oldest Old Demdike spoke again. "If all the Dead are willing, the Demdike sisters will not stand in the way. But there are four Demdike puppets and only three Demdike sisters. I myself will play Elizabeth."

The second oldest chimed in, "I will play Alison Demdike."

The third said, "I will be Jennet, the youngest and sweetest."

The three turned to Old Mistress Demdike with malicious grins on their faces.

"Who will play Old Demdike? Who will have that honour?"

They all three cackled, as though at some private joke at Old Demdike's expense. The gathering fell silent. The Spirits of the Dead looked at each other and away again. Not one would look at Old Demdike. It seemed that she had done nothing to endear herself to any of them. Jennet slipped her hand into Emmet's. He squeezed her cold fingers.

"Poor Granny," Jennet whispered, "surely someone will help her."

She looked up at him, her green eyes awash with tears. Emmet couldn't think of a single thing to do or say. The silence was broken by a furious roar from Old Demdike herself. She shouted a string of magic words and pointed her pipe towards the puppets. There was a blinding flash, a terrible noise and much smoke. Lily screamed, and the Spirits of the Dead moaned, fearfully. When the smoke cleared, to the astonishment and horror of the Company, Old Demdike's puppet likeness was on fire, burned away almost to nothing. Mistress Alice spoke in horrified tones.

"Oh, my dear Mistress Demdike, what have you done?"

Old Demdike glared round at them all defiantly. Her hideous face was black with soot. She looked terrifying in her rage.

"Mistress Demdike will play Mistress Demdike! Have you all forgotten that one of our number must remain with the

124

puppets to maintain the Glamour?"

There was a stunned silence.

Aunt Salome was the first to recover from the shock. She spoke with grudging admiration.

"This is a brave thing you do. It may also be the last. Are you prepared to die for The Company of the Silver Hare? And do you have the power to hold the Glamour for the length of time this will take?"

The oldest Demdike sister stepped forward and made a sound like a creaking gate. She was clearing her throat.

"She will not be alone. We still have our powers, yes, even in the grave we hold them, and the Demdike sisters are a force to be reckoned with yet."

The Silver Hare had not spoken for some time. Now it raised its head and regarded Old Demdike and the three old sisters steadily.

"For whom do you this? For the Path of Light or for your own dark ends?"

"We do it," said the youngest Demdike sister, with great dignity, "for True Love."

There was a rustle like a collective sigh from the Spirits of the Dead. "True Love, True Love," they whispered wistfully. "Yes," Old Demdike spoke in gentler tones. "My Granddaughter, my Scarlet Flower, is a True Lover. And the boy she loves is one of the Chosen. We see this clearly now. Behold!"

She pointed her charred pipe at Jennet and Emmet, sitting side by side on the silken cushions, still holding hands. Everyone turned to look at them. Emmet wanted the ground to open up and swallow him. He could feel himself burning fiery red with embarrassment.

"Emmet," Lily squeaked excitedly, "you're glowing! So is Jennet. What does it mean?"

Emmet and Jennet looked at each other helplessly then down at their linked fingers. It was true, a rosy glow appeared all around them.

"It is the Aura," said The Silver Hare, gravely. "The Aura

of True Love!"

Hot beyond bearing now, Emmet unconsciously put up his free hand and swept the hair from his sticky forehead. A gasp went up from Spirits and Faery Clans alike.

"The Star of the Chosen!"

Great excitement bordering on pandemonium broke out in the silken tent. Everyone seemed to be talking at once. After a few moments, The Silver Hare put up its paw for silence.

"True Love and The Choosing," it said. "It is unusual but not unknown for the two to go together. The last it happened to I believe, was you, Atterlothe, five hundred and thirty one year ago at Imbolc." It glanced at Atterlothe who inclined his head. "And you," it continued, "became the Elven King."

Wayland Smith spoke anxiously, "But they are children, Lord, only children. Emmet has no Faery blood in his veins. How can this be?"

"As yet," said The Silver Hare, "we do not need to know. But for both the Smith and the Demdike families it is a great honour. And," its silvery glance rested on Old Demdike and her ghostly ancestors, "a chance for one who has strayed to step once more onto the path of light."

The Chovihani rose from the cushion and her gold hoop earrings sparkled in the light of Emmet's star.

"Much is settled," she announced in her abrupt way. "Our course of action is agreed. The finer details cannot be arranged until events unfold. This night, All Souls Night, belongs to the Dead. Let us join with them in their celebrations."

There was eager assent from the Spirits of the Dead, and soon a rather strange party was in full swing. It seemed odd to the children to celebrate without food, but although the Dead could no longer eat, they could most certainly dance, and this they proceeded to do with gay abandon, kicking up their tattered heels and clattering their bones to ghostly music obligingly played by the Faery musicians.

Emmet and Jennet sat awkwardly together in a corner, watching the dancers. Ma trod a graceful measure with Charlie, Hetty and Letty spun in mad circles with Billy, and

Lily held one of old Mrs. Law's babies, jiggling it up and down in time to the music.

"Emmet," said Jennet after an anxious silence, "did you know I was your Own True Love?" Her heart thumped painfully in her rib cage as she waited for his answer. "Emmet?" she poked him irritably in the ribs.

"Ow! Don't poke, Jennet. I'm young. What do I know about True Love?"

Jennet felt tears prickle at the back of her eyes. She wanted to slap him.

"You must know how you feel about me, surely? You do like me, don't you?"

He answered quietly, and she had to strain to hear him above the music and laughter.

"Since I met you, my life has changed completely. You are the person I want to see when I wake up in the morning. I want to be near you in the day. I want to tell you all the things I think about. I like your red hair and your green eyes. I dream about you at night, and you smell nice. That's how I feel about you. "Is that True Love?"

Lit only by Emmet's star and their shared pink glow, Jennet answered, "I think it's probably enough to be going on with."

15. A SHOCK FOR ROGER NOWELL

Things went rather flat for a week or so after All Souls Night. Ma, who knew that she could not see her older children until the following summer, was silent and ill-tempered. It was cold, dark and miserable at the front and back ends of the day. The girls found it harder and harder to leave their warm beds in the mornings and Saffron had de-camped back to the Faery Realms.

"For the winter," she explained. "It's too cold here. I will come and visit you when the cold departs."

"You are a fair-weather faery," grumbled Letty.

"That's right," Saffron grinned cheerfully, and vanished in a whirl of faery dust.

No one mentioned True Love, as it clearly made Emmet and Jennet uncomfortable, and although the star shone faintly beneath Emmet's fringe, he seemed no closer to seeing the faery horse again. The one good thing which seemed to have happened was Old Demdike's apparent forgiveness of her Scarlet Flower. She took to appearing from time to time down the chimney of the Smith's cottage in her raven form to smoke a pipe of tobacco with Pa and partake of a glass of methyglyn. She said little, but treated the grandchildren with her old fierce affection and, after a few weeks, Jennet and Jimmy took to visiting Malkin Tower, their family home, on Sundays again. Lily was curious about these visits.

"Can't we come, too?" she asked, as Jennet and Jimmy were about to set off. Jennet shook her head and Jimmy looked uncomfortable.

"Not like here," he said. "Not good place for my Lily to go. Stay here with Ma and Pa. Jimmy and my Jennet soon be home."

"But why?" Lily was persistent. "I haven't met your Ma, not to speak to. And I like Alison. Why can't we come?"

"Leave them be, Lily," said Ma firmly, seeing the anxiety on Jennet and Jimmy's faces. "I've jobs for you to do here."

She handed Jimmy a large basket. "Some comforts for your Granny and your Ma. There's a rabbit pie, some of Henny Penny's eggs, a pot of honey and tea wrapped in that handkerchief."

Jennet's eyes widened. Tea was almost unheard of in England and worth a king's ransom.

"Aunt Salome gave it to me. Tell your granny to use it sparingly. Bring me back the basket and tell her she can bring the pie dish next time she visits."

Jennet kissed Ma's cheek by way of a thank you, and brother and sister were out of the cottage door, scuttling off up the path before Lily could say anything else.

"Lily," said Ma, gently, "Malkin Tower is not a nice place. It's dirty and squalid and broken. Jennet and Jimmy love their family, but they are ashamed of where they come from. Please don't embarrass them by asking again. Come now, its time to go to Church."

It was a bitterly cold day, and the Smith family wrapped themselves up as well as they could for the long walk. The vicar greeted them at the church door.

"Ah, Master Smith, Mistress, your family is growing apace, is it not?" He lowered his voice slightly. "And the Demdike brats, do they serve you well?"

Ma bobbed him a curtsey, her eyes expressionless.

"Indeed, they do, Vicar. Short rations and regular beatings, as you recommended, works wonders, I find. Thank you for your most excellent advice."

"Not at, not at all, Mistress."

The vicar looked shiftily from side to side and lowered his voice even further, although they were the first to arrive. Emmet thought he looked rather like a ferret with his long and pointed nose and mean, shifty eyes.

"I ask, because rumours are rife in the village, you know. They do say Old Mistress Demdike and her daughter have the evil eye. Cows have been overlooked, and there have been deaths," he looked half fearfully over his shoulder, "which cannot be explained."

"Surely, Vicar," Pa spoke in deferential tones, but there was a steely glint in his eye, "an educated man of God pays no credence to such tales?"

"No, indeed," the vicar said hastily. "Tales, of course. But no smoke without fire, as the saying goes. I was dining with Magistrate Roger Nowell only last week…"

Here he gave Pa a sly look to see if he was impressed.

"A sound man indeed, says he won't tolerate witchcraft in his parish. Keen, you know, very keen. May have to make examples, he says."

"How interesting, Vicar," said Ma calmly, her voice sounding as though she was not interested at all. "Do keep us informed of any developments, will you not? Girls, come inside with me. The vicar cannot spend all his valuable time talking to us. We must share him with the rest of his flock. We eagerly await your sermon, sir."

She swept him a devastating curtsey, so low that her hood almost swept the floor, and flounced past him into the church. Villagers were beginning to arrive, and the Vicar turned his attention to greeting them. Mistress Alice glided up the aisle of the church, pausing by the Smith's pew.

"And so it begins," she said, in a voice barely louder than a whisper, not looking at Ma.

"Take heart," Ma murmured gently, "all may yet be well."

Then in louder tones, "Good day, Mistress Nutter. I have completed the lace that you ordered. Perhaps we might call on you in Roughlee hall this afternoon?"

"Delightful," returned Mistress Alice. "I await your visit with much eagerness."

It was so cold on the journey home that Emmet felt his bones ache, especially his toes and fingers which managed to be both numb and painful at the same time.

"Must we go to Mistress Alice's?" grumbled Hetty after they had drunk hot soup and had a nip of methyglyn. "My toes have only just thawed out. Can't we stay here by the fire?"

"Certainly not." Ma was firm. "Mistress Alice is expecting us. Hurry up and get yourselves ready. I do not wish

130

to keep her waiting."

The family reluctantly left the warmth of their cottage for the second time that day. A freezing wind had sprung up which hit them with an icy blast.

"Can't we change, Ma?" begged Lily. "We shan't mind the cold in our hare forms, and it will be so much quicker…ple-e-se!"

Everyone gazed at her hopefully.

"There's not a soul abroad," Pa offered tentatively.

It was true. The whole village of Barley was indoors trying to keep warm after their bitter excursion to church. Ma wavered. Finally, she said,. "Alright, but at least wait until we reach the meadow."

The change was effortless. Emmet thought gratefully of all the hours Jennet had spent patiently training him as they sped across the bleak countryside, Lily and the twins turning joyous somersaults as they went.

As they approached Roughlee Hall, they observed a big black horse tethered beside the front wall, steam rising from its body and nostrils as it champed in the freezing air.

"Stop!" Emmet heard Ma's voice clearly in his mind. "That is the magistrate's horse. Do not change! Do not move."

The six brown hares crouched motionless in the barren winter earth. A casual observer might have taken them for clods or stones. As they watched from their vantage point of some twenty feet away, the front door of the hall opened and Roger Nowell strode out. His face was pale with rage. Framed in the doorway stood Alice Nutter with her maid Anne Chattox who seemed to be supporting her mistress. The Magistrate turned to face them.

"I will have my way!" he shouted furiously. "Do not imagine you can defy me forever."

Mistress Nutter said something in reply, too low for the watchers to hear. Whatever it was seemed to enrage Nowell beyond bearing for he lost control completely, lunged forward and seized Mistress Alice by her hair, throwing her to the ground. Anne gave a piercing scream whilst Emmet and the others watched in horror and disbelief.

Without warning, a bolt of lightening shot from the hares, hitting Roger Nowell full in the chest. He staggered backwards, trying to right himself but it was followed by another bolt and another, sending him sprawling across the grass. There was complete silence as Anne and Mistress Alice gazed at their fallen tormentor, mouths open in astonishment.

Roger Nowell lay still as death where he had fallen, and for a second or two, it seemed as if he truly must have been killed, but a shudder passed though his large frame and he struggled to his feet. His face was twisted with a curious mixture of rage and terror and had turned a greenish shade of white. He pointed a shaking finger at the frightened women.

"Witches!" he screamed hoarsely. "Don't think I don't know what you are! You're a pair of witches and I'll see you hanged, and your bloody coven with you."

Scarcely knowing what she did, Anne made a move as though to help him, but he backed away from her.

"Don't touch me, you hag! I'll see you burn, first. Witches!"

The magistrate struggled onto his horse, and for the second time, the Smith family watched him galloping ignominiously away from Roughlee Hall. Not until he had completely vanished from view did Ma give the order, "Change!"

Back in their human forms, Ma, Pa and the children rushed to the aid of Mistress Alice who seemed too shocked to move. Pa picked her up unceremoniously in his huge arms and carried her into the house, laying her gently on a large settle in the great cave-like kitchen. Anne hurried to bring a mug of warm methyglyn to her mistress and Alice Nutter sipped it gratefully.

"Thank you, my dear," she said, gently. "It has perhaps made things worse, but still, I thank you."

Ma stared at her, uncomprehending.

"For what do you thank me, Mistress? I did nothing."

Mistress Alice looked confused.

"For the lightening bolts. I assume it was your work? If not you?" Her eyes swivelled to Pa's face. Wayland Smith shook his head slowly. Everyone looked at the four children standing frightened and shivering by the fire.

"It was me."

Lily spoke in a small voice.

There was a stunned silence, broken at last by Ma.

"You, Lily?"

Lily's chubby face went red.

"I didn't do it on purpose, Ma. I didn't know I was going to do it... it was just... when that man tried to hurt Mistress Alice, it just sort of happened, I don't know how. I got all hot and everything went red." She looked at Ma anxiously. "I didn't mean to, Ma. Was it bad?"

"Oh, Lily!" Ma enfolded the girl in her arms and rocked her gently.

"It wasn't bad, Lily, but it was dangerous."

"Because I might have killed Master Nowell?" Lily's voice had gone from small to tiny.

"Well, that too, I suppose, but because he believes Anne and Mistress Alice to be witches, and now he has proof."

Strangely, however, Roger Nowell made no move against Mistress Alice. Lily was distraught at first over her slip of magical vengeance, but as the days went by and there was no witch-hunt and no arrests, her sunny nature reasserted itself.

"P'raps he's forgotten?" she wondered, but Ma and Pa were under no such illusions and exchanged troubled glances.

"Roger Nowell does not forget," Ma observed darkly. "He is biding his time, that is all. Why, I cannot think. But in the mean time, you, Lily, in fact all of you need more practice in magic. Much, much more, particularly as regards self control."

Atterlothe winked at them behind Ma's back. It was a dark evening in mid-December, and he had come to visit them and smoke a pipe of tobacco with Wayland Smith. Pa shook his head at him in reproof, but he had a twinkle in his eye as he looked at his friend.

"It wants only a week until the Winter Solstice,"

Atterlothe said gravely, "and in light of recent events, we shall not celebrate at Roughlee Hall." He hesitated whilst he knocked out his pipe on the hearth. "Why not come you all instead to the Faery Realms?"

Emmet almost stopped breathing. The image of the faery foal he carried always in his heart sprang into his minds eye. Lately, she had also cantered through his dreams at night.

"Please, please, please," he whispered under his breath.

There was a long silence whilst Ma seemed to be considering.

"Thank you, Atterlothe. We shall be honoured and delighted. I should love to see dear Savine again. It has been too long. But," she fixed him with a stern gaze, "the no-time-at-all-has-gone rule must apply."

Atterlothe bowed gracefully. "Of course. It shall be as you wish."

Over the next week, the days grew shorter and shorter. The sun, when it was visible at all, seemed almost too weary to raise its head above the horizon, and by four o'clock it was quite dark again. Food was not so plentiful, and the Smith family was glad of Ma's skills and forethought in all the salting and drying and pickling she had done in the autumn. The forge, as the warmest place in the village, was full of a constant procession of visitors who came on the smallest pretext and stayed as long as they dared. Pa working away at his anvil was oblivious to conversation as the rhythmical clanging of his hammer drowned out most of it, but Jimmy and Emmet caught many snippets of gossip from the old wives of the village, and what they heard was disturbing.

"…dead and nothing wrong with him the day before!"

"…milk sour, overlooked, I'd say."

"…a poppet with pins in it, the image of the magistrate. Found in a hole in the wall."

"…must be witchcraft. Witches in our midst, you mark my words."

Ma finally put a stop to the gossipers by setting a simple repelling charm at the door of the smithy which had the effect

134

of sending them home slightly bemused to their own meagre firesides. The talk of witchcraft made everyone jumpy and anxious, however, and Ma and Pa worried about it long after the children had gone to their beds.

"Surely Old Demdike is not fool enough to still be making her poppets after all that's happened?" Ma wondered.

Wayland Smith shook his head. "She's not a fool. My belief is that someone is starting rumours. Someone is setting the scene for a witch hunt."

Ma looked up from her lace making. The candlelight lit her face from below, throwing the lines and planes into sharp relief.

"Roger Nowell."

Pa puffed at his pipe. "He wishes to catch more than one fish. He is after the shoal."

His wife bit her lip and there was fear in her eyes. "That is why he has made no move against Mistress Alice. Oh Wayland, is there nothing we can do to stop it?"

The Smith gently took her hand. "Nothing, my dear. We have put in motion all that we can. It is in the lap of the Great Mother."

On the day of the Winter Solstice, there was an air of great expectancy among the children. Lily and the twins could hardly contain themselves with the thought of seeing Speedwell and Savine once more.

"I'm going to have green hair, this time," announced Lily. Her face puckered in a worried frown. "I do hope I can remember how to fly."

"How do you suppose we shall get there?" Jennet was thoughtful. "If we go through Pa's breast plate, how will Pa get there?"

"I don't like going through Pa's middle," said Lily. "It frightens me."

"Don't worry, Lily. We shall go a different way this time. Are you all ready?"

Ma picked up a small package containing a beautiful piece of lace she had created for the Elven Queen. "Come, children.

Henny Penny, are you coming?"

Henny Penny rose from her basket by the fire and fluffed her feathers. "Of course," she clucked, cheerfully, "a change is as good as a rest."

Jimmy lifted her in his arms and they all followed Ma and Pa into the forge. Ma cast a circle and freshened up the repelling charm. Wayland Smith put on his helmet and breastplate and Lily swallowed nervously, holding tight to Jimmy's hand. Pa picked up a silver horseshoe and set it carefully on its prongs so that it stood up by itself in the centre of the floor. Ma pointed at the horseshoe and chanted a string of strange words. The horseshoe seemed at first to wobble, then it began to grow. It grew until it was the size of an archway. Mistress Smith turned to the children.

"Do you have your amulets?" They all nodded. "Then hold hands and follow me."

She took Lily's hand and they formed a human chain, Jimmy last with Henny Penny tucked under his arm. Ma stopped through the archway leading them all behind her. They blinked in surprise as they found themselves in what appeared to be a dark tunnel lit only by a thin rectangle of light outlining a door at the end. When they reached it, the door revealed itself to be a heavy tapestry curtain which Ma slid across, and they stepped out into Savine's outside room.

The Elven King and Queen were seated on one of the divans and rose to meet their guests with beaming faces. Savine embraced Mistress Smith with warm delight.

"My dear, it has been so long, too long by half. We must not let so much time pass us by again." She turned to Pa. "Wayland, it is so good to see all of you, to have you back again. The castle felt quite empty without you, and Speedwell cried for a whole week. Your children," she turned again to Ma and Pa, "are a delight and a credit to you. All your children." Savine spoke with emphasis and put an arm around the shoulders of Jimmy and Jennet. Lily flung her arms around the Elven Queen's slender waist and buried her face in the soft folds of her gown.

136

"We missed you too. Please, where is Speedwell?"

"She does not know that you were coming," said Atterlothe. "We thought it would be a wonderful surprise for her. I believe her to be in her bedchamber. Would you like to go and find her?"

Hetty, Letty and Lily needed no second bidding. They scampered off excitedly and delighted shrieks could be heard from another part of the castle. Jennet looked around the familiar room. All was she remembered, apart from one thing. Instead of being open to the sky, it seemed to be covered by a crystal dome which glittered as the weak sunlight caught it. Atterlothe followed her gaze.

"We have winter here, just as you do," he said. "Brighter and not as harsh as in the human lands, but cold nonetheless. Wayland, will you take a glass of mead?"

Savine moved gracefully toward a small table bearing a flask and delicate, engraved glasses.

"I am so overcome to see you all. I am forgetting my manners."

She poured a glass for everyone and added to it some Liquid Life Force. "We must be sure to keep your memories intact."

For a few moments there was a flurry of commotion as the glasses were handed around, and all were seated. Atterlothe raised his glass.

"To the Winter Solstice and," he added, "to safe passage through the dark times ahead."

"Amen to that," Wayland said fervently, and they all drank deeply. For a moment there was a silence. Emmet felt the Liquid Life Force lighting up his insides. The star upon his forehead tingled. Pooka. He could contain himself no longer.

"Please, Atterlothe," there was a note of desperation in his voice as he spoke. He swallowed anxiously, "When can I see Pooka?"

"Emmet, what am I thinking of? You must be aching to see her. We shall go at once. Wayland, would you care to accompany us?" Atterlothe rose and bowed courteously to Ma,

137

Savine and Jennet. "Ladies, please excuse us."

Pa and Emmet accompanied him out of the garden room, in the direction of the meadow. Emmet's heart felt ready to burst with excitement and his blood thundered in his ears. He heard her voice in his mind, before he saw her.

"Emmet, you are come."

The star blazed on his forehead. He broke into a run. The meadow seemed to rush towards him. The Old Oak Dryads bade him kindly welcome but he paid them no heed. She was there, cantering towards him, her star blazing as brightly as his. She had grown. She was beautiful.

Pooka.

Their foreheads touched, the stars fused together. Emmet's brain flooded with light. There were no words, just completeness. Pooka. Emmet.

Wayland Smith and Atterlothe stopped by the Oak Dryads and watched them. Both had tears in their eyes.

"Will you look at those young ones," one of the Oak Dryads rumbled affectionately. "Does my old heart good to see it, it does."

Stella trotted up to see them, delighted. "My liege, thank you for bringing Emmet. My child has been pining for him. My dear Wayland," she nuzzled his cheek affectionately.

Pa blew his nose loudly. "Stella. It has been a long time. And you still have your diamond shoes. Well, well." His voice was unsteady. "So your child has chosen mine. I do not pretend to understand this, but I am delighted and honoured. And," this last was almost to himself, "a little afraid."

The Winter Solstice seemed to Jennet to be the most beautiful of all the celebrations she had experienced in her short life. All were there - Aunt Salome and the Egyptians, the Chattoxes, the Demdikes, all the Faery Clans and Mistress Alice, serene as always, and, on the face of it at least, quite recovered from her ordeal at the hands of Roger Nowell.

Atterlothe had conjured another crystal dome to cover the entire orchard, and it was as warm as a summer's day. Stella and Pooka were there with Emmet always in attendance, and many other magical birds and beasts. The Silver Hare presided over the festivities with its customary benevolence.

There was the usual feasting, music and dancing, and incredible fireworks which the children had never seen before and which Lily, until she had got used to them, found rather frightening. Ma seemed gentler and more relaxed in the Faery Realms and made no comment at all when her daughters fluttered awkwardly about on their borrowed wings with wild, multi-coloured hair.

After the festival was over, and the Clans and the Company of the Silver Hare began to disperse, The Elven King urged the Smith family to stay.

"Rest here a while, Wayland," he said. "Let your family have a holiday. The dark times are almost upon us. It is written in the stars, and the Wild Hunt are abroad almost nightly now. Stay and gather your energies. Let the children enjoy the time they have left together."

Wayland Smith looked questioningly at his wife. She nodded slightly. The two of them glanced towards Emmet and Jennet who sat close together by one of the fires which still burned brightly in the orchard. The flames lit up Jennet's wild red hair as she leaned towards Emmet to say something. Around the two of them, the pink aura of True Love was clearly visible. Close by, Stella and Pooka cropped the grass contentedly.

"We will stay for a while at least," said Ma. "I have been speaking with Savine. She has offered to give the children an intensive course in magic. It is so dangerous at home – we have to snatch moments when we can, and progress is slow. I do not know if they realize that when the dark times come, they will be parted. I cannot bring myself to talk to them about it."

Atterlothe was silent for a moment, his green eyes troubled.

"What the future holds for them I do not know," he said at last, "but Emmet is one of the Chosen and they are True Lovers. I cannot believe they will not be together in the end."

A strange sound broke from the lips of Wayland Smith who turned abruptly and walked away into the darkness. Atterlothe raised a questioning eyebrow at Mistress Smith. A look of deep distress came over her face, and her eyes filled with tears.

"Have you forgotten, Atterlothe," she said sadly, "that Wayland lost his own True Love many centuries ago when the world was young. Her name was Herva and she was a swan woman. She put on her wings and flew away one morning. He never understood why she left him and he never saw her again. He told me this when we first met."

Atterlothe was stricken with remorse. "My dear, forgive me. I had forgotten, you are right. But that was long ago and I know that he loves you dearly."

Mistress Smith said, somewhat sadly, "I am his dear love, yes; his True Love, no. He and she, they are immortal but I shall one day join my children in the graveyard. So you see, just because Emmet and Jennet are True Lovers does not necessarily follow that they will have a happy ending."

Savine appeared noiselessly beside them and slipped her arm thought Ma's.

"We must trust and believe that all shall be well." Her warm honey voice was full of reassurance. "Do not dwell on grief and sadness. Tonight is the darkest night and the shortest day of the year. It is natural that you should feel low. Give it no credence. Tomorrow the days begin to lengthen and the light to return. Atterlothe, I think we all need some Liquid Life Force."

The next day, lessons began in earnest. Savine was a gentle and patient teacher and knew exactly how to get the best from her pupils.

"Hetty and Letty, you are doing marvellously well. I am very pleased with you. Your knowledge of herb lore is excellent. I see your mother's influence here. Well done.

"Lily, you need you work harder at the circle casting – that last one was sloppy. I know it seems basic, but it is one of the most important spells you will ever learn. I know you can do it, dear.

"Jennet, that was excellent flying. Remember, the broomstick is simply something to sit on – a stool would do just as well. But you must be fully invisible first. I could see your hair that time. Try it again, please."

Jimmy, despite his seeming simplicity, mastered everything he was taught effortlessly. One of his greatest skills was Changing, and not only into a hare. To everyone's surprise, he was able to assume the likeness of anything or anyone, at will.

"This is truly a gift from the Great Mother, Jimmy. Use it only for good purposes. Used lightly, it can be dangerous. All right, children, that is enough for today. Have a rest or go and play."

Being sent to rest or play was quite a novelty for the human children. Most of their time at home was taken up with the work of garden and smithy, which at times seemed relentless. In contrast, Speedwell seemed to have to do little but care for her goats, and this she did with great tenderness, brushing their silky hair and making sure they had only the choicest food.

As the adored only child of the Elven King and Queen, she was perhaps too used to having her own way, and although she could do no wrong in the eyes of Lily, Hetty and Letty could see that she was rather spoilt.

Saffron had taken up residence on Speedwell's bedroom windowsill. Instead of a pad of sheep's wool, Speedwell had supplied her with her own miniature four-poster bed lined with swans down and hung with silken coverlets. Letty eyed it admiringly.

"You won't want to come home again when the weather gets warmer. It's too nice here."

Saffron surprised them. "Yes, I will. I've missed the cottage. I'll be glad to come back."

"But it is so wonderful here," said Hetty, "how can you possibly want to leave?"

The faery shrugged her tiny shoulders. "It isn't home

though, is it?"

Some weeks had passed when one morning at breakfast Savine announced that her school of human children were well grounded in elementary magic and that she was satisfied with their progress.

"I am proud of you all," she beamed. "You have worked hard and achieved so much in such a short time. You must remember however," her tone was serious now, "that when you return to the human realms, magic must be used with care and secrecy, and only in cases of greatest need, if you are to live safely in your native land. Most humans are not blessed with your gifts, and it is in human nature to fear and hate that which they do not understand. Do not put yourselves at risk." The Elven Queen gazed at them, then her face relaxed. "Today is a special day. Before you return home, there will be an important ceremony."

She turned to Atterlothe, who continued. "You are all aware that Stella's foal has Chosen Emmet to be her lifelong companion, and that he has already given her the name Pooka. All this happened faster than has ever been known before. It is usual for there to be a naming ceremony, and so we shall hold it today, before you leave."

All this talk of going home had caught the children unawares.

"Also," said Atterlothe, "it is Wayland's task to shoe Pooka with her first pair of diamond shoes, and for Emmet to ride her the first time. She is big enough now. The year is turning and the stars tell me that the time is right."

Emmet blushed a deep crimson. Somehow, actually riding Pooka had never crossed his mind. It had seemed enough to feel that she was part of him. He did feel anxious, however. Although he loved horses dearly, he had never actually ridden one.

"Atterlothe," Emmet faltered, "I don't know how to ride. Will that matter? I'm sure I could learn."

The Elven King put a hand on his shoulder. "When the time comes, you will find that you already know. Pooka is no

142

ordinary horse, and she will help you, have no fear. However, I need to talk to you and your father before the ceremony. There is more to being Chosen than you are aware of, and you may, if you wish, reject the Choosing."

Emmet stared at him in consternation. Reject the Choosing? Renounce the bond with Pooka? He didn't think he could, even if he wanted to. It would be like tearing off one of his own limbs.

"Come," said Savine to Ma and the children, "we have much to prepare, and Atterlothe needs time alone with Emmet and Wayland."

She shepherded them all out of the room with her customary graceful authority. When they had gone, Atterlothe took his tobacco pouch from his scrip and offered it to Pa. They lit their pipes and puffed in silence.

"Emmet," The Elven King spoke at last, "what do you know about the Choosing?"

Emmet thought hard. "I know that it's special, and that it doesn't usually happen with humans."

Atterlothe glanced at Pa, fixed Emmet with an intense look and said, "There are always at any given time, twelve Chosen pairs, horses and riders, in the Faery Realms. When it is time for an old Chosen Pair to fade, a new Choosing will take place. This always happens, since time out of mind, no one knows how or why."

Emmet was struggling to understand. "What is fade?" He asked.

"The Faery Clans may live many hundreds, even thousands of years. We do not experience death in the way you humans do. Rather, if mortally sick or wounded, or in extreme old age, our life force grows weaker and we literally fade away until we vanish altogether. At the moment Pooka chose you, another pair faded, Cinquefoil and Starlight. They were old and their time had come."

"But Emmet is not one of the Faery people," said Wayland Smith. "His life span will be a normal human one, and when it is done, he will die."

143

Atterlothe sighed. "I am aware of this, old friend. The other thing you should know, Emmet, is that once you and Pooka are fully joined, if one of you should fade, or die in your case, the other will die too. Neither will be able to live without the other. Are you prepared for this?"

Emmet thought of life without Pooka. He shivered involuntarily.

"Yes."

"I knew that would be your answer," said Atterlothe. "One more thing. Do you know what the role of the Chosen is in the Faery Realms?"

Emmet shook his head.

"The Chosen are the guardians of the Faery Realms. They are the first on the battlefield should an enemy threaten, and the last to leave it. They are the defenders of all we hold dear, and their valour is legendary. Their honour is beyond question. Are you, a human boy who has not thirteen summers to his name, able to take on this role?"

There was a short silence. Emmet's head was in a whirl. He thought back to that far off day in early summer at Pendle Hill, the day he first met Jennet. He remembered the feeling he had experienced then, as though something had begun.

"I don't know if I'm able," he said at last, "but I'm willing to try my best." He looked doubtfully at Atterlothe and Pa. "Will that be enough?"

The Elven King replied, "No one can do more than their best, Emmet. And so long as my own life light shines brightly, you will never want for help."

The Naming ceremony was something Emmet would remember and marvel at for the rest of his life.

It was held on the jousting field behind the castle, and it seemed that all the Faery Clans had come to witness the event. The crowds were enormous and little silken tents in gay colours, pennants flapping in the frosty air, served warm food and mead under a bright blue sky.

The Ceremony itself was quite simple. First Wayland Smith shod the white mare with her diamond shoes, amid

144

delighted cheering from the crowds, on a raised platform so that everyone could see. On the platform were seated the Elven King and Queen, Figwort, The Silver Hare, The Five, and the Heads of all the faery Clans. Speedwell, as the Princess Royal, had her own box on one side, and the Smith and Demdike children sat with her, Henny Penny perched on Jimmy's shoulder so as to get a good view. Emmet sat with them in a daze. He had moments of complete unreality when he felt that all this must surely be a dream from which he would wake at any second. He also had moments of sheer terror in which his scalp prickled and his stomach churned. He was wrenched from his thoughts by Lily and Jennet poking him frantically.

"Go on, Emmet, you have to go up, they are calling for you. Go!"

For a split second, Emmet thought of running away, but the star on his forehead began to blaze and Pooka's voice spoke in his mind.

"Have no fear, Emmet, come to me. We are one, this is our time. Come to me."

The terror left him and he found himself striding purposefully out of the box and across the platform toward Pooka who stood waiting for him in front of Savine. The Elven King seemed to have disappeared, but Emmet had no time to ponder on this for the Silver Hare raised its paw, the crowd fell silent and Savine stepped forward.

"Emmet, son of Wayland, you have been Chosen. Do you accept this Choosing that will bind you both together until the end of time?"

"I do," Emmet cried out in a ringing voice.

"And do you accept that neither one shall live without the other, that her death shall be your death, and your death shall be hers?"

"I do."

"And do you most solemnly and joyfully swear to defend the Faery Realms in honour and bravery until the last breath you both shall take?"

"I do."

"Then Emmet, son of Wayland, tell us all her name."

"Pooka," said Emmet, loudly. "Her name is Pooka."

The crowd went crazy and a great roar arose, "Emmet, son of Wayland! Pooka! Pooka!"

For a full minute, the Silver Hare let the crowd have its way, then once again it raised its paw for silence.

"Emmet, son of Wayland," it said in its starry voice, "it is time for you to ride."

Afterwards, Emmet could not remember how he got onto Pooka's back. Perhaps he flew there, he could not say. All he knew was that he was there and it was the most natural and beautiful thing in all the world. He ran his fingers through her silvery mane and patted her warm neck.

"It this all right?" he said to her in his mind. "Am I hurting you?"

"Of course not. This is how it is meant to be."

Pooka trotted round to face the crowd which began to part. Up through the centre high-stepped eleven white faery horses with their riders seated proudly on their backs. At their head rode Atterlothe on Stella. The Chosen stopped and formed a semicircle in front of the platform.

"Pooka," Stella whinnied, "come ride with us."

"Emmet, son of Wayland," Atterlothe's voice shook with emotion, "come ride with us."

"Hold tight, Emmet."

Pooka took a flying leap into their midst, the Chosen wheeled around and galloped madly back down the field. Faster and faster they rode. The ecstatic crowd went wild once more, but the riders left the sound far behind as they galloped across the green meadowland, down to the sea. The hooves of the faery horses thundered, the surf breaking on the shore thundered, all Emmet's senses were reeling. He felt as though he was flying. Pooka's body felt part of his own. Where she wished to go, where he wished to go, all was the same. He smelled the sea and gazed in awe at the endless waters before him.

"To the air," cried a voice. He thought afterwards that it

was Atterlothe's. Emmet felt something pushing at his back. He twisted his head around and gasped. From Pooka's white back, from the backs of all the horses, were sprouting wings, enormous, muscular, silver tipped white wings.

And then they truly were flying. Over the sea, low at first so that the icy spray of the waves hit Emmet in the face and made him catch his breath, but quickly gaining height so that the faery realms spread away beneath them like one of Ma's patchwork quilts.

Higher and higher flew the Chosen, the land falling further away. The sky above grew darker, and constellations strange and new to Emmet began to shine out. There was a rushing and unmistakable ghostly baying of hounds. The Wild Hunt hove into view, streaming towards them, the mighty, antlered Hunter at the head, his wild eyes glittering, his teeth, white in the darkness of his face, bared in a fierce expression.

"Well met," he roared, and for a moment he gazed searchingly into Emmet's eyes. Emmet felt as though his soul had been laid bare. Perhaps the Hunter approved of what he read there, for he let out a shout of delight and tossed a leather bag into Emmet's lap.

"A gift," he roared again, above the baying of the hounds. "A gift for the young Fledglings, a naming gift."

Before Emmet had time to stutter his thanks, the Hunt faded away, just as he remembered from midsummer, and the Chosen, at a signal from Atterlothe, wheeled like a flock of birds and began their downward flight.

The celebrations on the jousting field lasted long into the night, but before the end, an exhausted Emmet took refuge in the orchard beyond Savine's garden room and sat by the bright fire with Pooka at his side, peacefully cropping the grass. Atterlothe slipped out of the shadows and joined him, sitting on a fallen log. He packed his pipe and smoked in silence. Emmet raised his head and looked at Atterlothe. "What will happen now?"

"You are officially one of the Chosen and are entitled to remain here in the Faery Realms. But you are also human and

147

have a home and life in the world of men. Pooka cannot live with you there – it would not be safe for any of you. For the time being, you must go home with your family to the forge and finish growing up."

"What about Pooka?"

"You can come and be with her whenever you wish. Indeed you must. You will need much training as a Chosen Pair. I do not pretend to understand this Choosing; all I know is that it is never wrong. The fact that you are human makes no difference. Somehow, the way will become clear. And in the meantime use your amulet."

"How?"

"When you lie down at night to sleep, hold it to your star, and call to Pooka. You will find yourself in the Faery Realms. Do this at night and, when you return, no time at all will have elapsed. Then you will sleep. This will stop you from becoming disorientated between the two worlds. When you wake in the morning, your time with Pooka will be like a vivid dream."

"Thank you, Atterlothe, for everything."

16. The Hooded Figure

The Forge was exactly as they had left it. When they emerged from the horseshoe arch, it dwindled to its normal size and toppled over, spinning and clattering to the floor. The fire still burned merrily in the cottage, the log Pa put on it before they left had not even caught the flames.

"This is so hard to get used to," declared Lily, wrinkling her nose. "We've been away for weeks but here it is, the same moment. I don't like it," she cried, and burst into tears.

Pa picked her up and set her on his knee.

"Don't cry, Lilykins. Ma, have you got the bottle that Savine gave you?"

Mistress Smith took a small crystal bottle from the folds of her gown and poured everyone a tot of Liquid Life Force. They immediately felt better. The time they'd spent In the Faery Realms began to recede in memory and home felt more real, more present. Life resumed its usual pattern, the boys helping Pa in the forge, the girls working with Ma. There was little to be done in the garden at this time of year and much of the daylight hours were spent in spinning and lace making. Everyday the girls and Ma wrapped themselves up warmly and went for a brisk walk to gather kindling for the forge. They were returning from one of these excursions with frozen fingers and running noses when a small pony and trap came clattering down the lane that led to the forge. Pa and Emmet came out to see who it could be.

"Mistress Alice!" Lily dropped her bundle of sticks and scampered up. "Why have you got your beehives with you?"

The back of the small trap was full of hives. Emmet stepped forward and took the pony's reins whilst Pa lifted Mistress Alice down from the trap. She tried to appear cheerful but her usually serene face was white and drawn.

"I have brought them to live at the forge, Lily. I have talked with the Royal Family and your mother will be the new Bee Mistress."

Lily stared. "But Mistress Alice, you love your bees so much, why do you want them to give them away?"

Mistress Alice's eyes filled with tears and her voice shook.

"The dark times are almost upon us. I do not expect to be at Roughlee Hall when the summer comes. It is important for me to know that my bees are safe and loved."

Hetty and Letty each slipped a hand into hers, leaning their heads against her shoulders in silent sympathy.

"Come in, Mistress, and drink a glass of mead. The boys will take the hives into the garden, and we will take most tender care of them, rest assured."

Ma led her friend inside the cottage; the children felt a sharp edge of unease.

Yuletide had come and gone, as had the Feast of Imbolc. The light was returning but it was still bitterly cold. Towards the end of February, Pa had taken upon himself, in addition to his work as village Smith, a new role, that of assisting the elderly sexton of the church with the grave digging.

"It will be useful," he said, "when the time comes."

He did not say what time he was referring to and the children did not press him. It was something that they did not wish to dwell upon too deeply.

March blew in with icy winds, flattening the early daffodils in Ma's garden. Jennet often neglected the work Ma set her to do in order to be by Emmet's side. She seemed almost glued to him like a shadow. Sometimes he woke in the night to see her sitting huddled by his pallet, wrapped in her shawl, her feet blue with cold and her white face pinched with misery.

"Go back to your bed, Jennet. You shouldn't be here. You're frozen."

He had been riding Pooka on the golden shore of the Faery Realms and his mind was still half with her. He closed his eyes for a moment and when he opened them, Jennet had gone.

One night, the Smiths were seated around the warm hearth when they heard coughing and spluttering in the wide chimney. A heavy soot fall almost put out the fire, and a large black raven, singed and choking, half-hopped, half-staggered out of the fireplace, turning instantly into Old Demdike. She was scarlet in the face and gasping for breath. She seemed more dead than alive. Ma and Pa rose swiftly and assisted her to a chair.

"Quickly, Hetty, fetch some water."

"Nay," wheezed Old Demdike, her red-rimmed eyes streaming, "something stronger."

Pa produced a mug of methyglyn and Ma laced it with Liquid Life Force. Old Demdike took a deep draught and leaned back in the chair with her eyes closed. Her breathing grew calmer. She took out her pipe but her old hands were shaking so badly that she could not fill it. Pa gently took it from her, packed it and lit it. She inhaled gratefully, puffed for a minute or two and took another swig of methyglyn. All were silent, waiting. At last she turned and faced them.

"They've got Alison."

"Who has Alison?"

"Master Nowell." She spat in the hearth venomously. "Says she's overlooked a peddler or some such nonsense. The story goes that she tried to beg some pins from him – that's a lie for a start. My Alison does have no need to beg. John Law, from Halifax. I know of him and his son Abraham, thick with Roger Nowell…" (Here she spat again) "…so they are. Says he refused her the pins and she set a curse on him, made him ill. A stroke they say, or a seizure." She snorted loudly, blowing soot onto Ma's clean apron. "Too much ale, more like. It was Abraham brought the charges."

Old Demdike was silent, gazing into the fire absently. Nobody spoke. She turned to them again, her eyes wet with tears. Angrily she wiped the tears away, smearing her face with soot. It looked comical, but no one laughed. Jennet thought of her pretty, smiling sister. She climbed onto her grandmother's lap and wound her arms around her neck in silent sympathy. Old Demdike clasped her fiercely.

"My Alison, she be a good girl. She would never do such

a thing – not but that she wouldn't know how, mind, but she has a kind heart. Nay, it's Mistress Alice he is after, but he'll take us all down first, all us ones the village believe are guilty, Demdikes and Chattoxes all. He'll take us first and he'll add her on, like she be an afterthought, and then…" Here she paused and spat for a third time. "…he will have killed all the witches,"

she spoke the hated word defiantly, glaring round as she said it, "and got Roughlee Hall, which is what he wanted all along."

Pa stood up and laid a large hand on her shoulder.

"We must call a meeting of the Company. Someone must meet with the Spirits of the Dead. Be not afraid, Mistress, our plans have been laid this many months. All is in readiness."

Old Demdike looked him in the eye.

"I'm not afraid, Master Smith. I'm guilty. This is my fault, and we all know it. The Silver Hare has always known it. I have given Roger Nowell the ammunition that he needed, by my dark ways - aye, as surely as if I'd placed it in his hand. It was one thing to know this time was coming, but to know it is here…well…" Her voice trailed off.

Ma spoke angrily. "Mistress Demdike, stop feeling sorry for yourself, for goodness sake. What's done is done. We are prepared and we will do that which is needful. But just you spit on my clean floor one more time and I'll give you something to be sorry for."

The Company met that night at Roughlee Hall under the cover of darkness. All arrived by magical means and careful Mistress Smith had woven so many repelling spells and circles of protection around the old house that it was doubtful even a flea could have got through uninvited. The Silver Hare and all The Five sat on their usual carved chairs with the children, Figwort, Saffron and other representatives of the Faery Clans around the table. The only person missing was the Elven King.

"Where is Atterlothe?" The Silver Hare asked.

Aunt Salome shifted in her chair. "He will be here directly, my Lord. There is some important business to which

152

he is attending."

Almost as she finished speaking, there was a brilliant flash of light, the universe shuddered and Atterlothe appeared before them, his arm around a cloaked figure.

"My apologies to the Company," he said in his easy way, "for my late arrival. I bring someone who I think you would like to see."

The cloak was whisked away and underneath stood Alison Demdike. Her usually pink and cheerful face was pale and showed the marks of tears, but otherwise she seemed unharmed. There was a stunned silence then everyone began to talk at once.

"Alison, are you all right?"

"Did they hurt you?"

"How did you do it, Atterlothe?"

The Silver Hare raised its paw for silence.

"Let the Elven King speak. Child, be seated. You look exhausted."

Alison sank gratefully into the chair that Pa brought for her, and laid her head on the table as though her neck could scarcely hold it up. Mistress Alice took her hand and stroked it gently. All heads turned expectantly to Atterlothe who sat down beside Pa.

"First of all, I beg your forgiveness for acting alone, but as soon as the news of Alison reached me, I knew that speed was of the essence. I had Saffron go to Read Hall to find out where Alison was being held and then it was but a small matter to wake the Old Demdike sisters, animate Alison's puppet and make the exchange during the night."

"It was neatly done, Atterlothe" said the Silver Hare, "but who will hold the Glamour?"

"The Old Ones still have considerable power of their own, my Lord. The second Old Demdike, can, I believe, hold it for a time. However, from what Alison tells me, and from what Saffron has overheard, I do not think she will be alone for long."

Mistress Demdike's head shot up sharply and she turned

153

as white as paper.

"Go on," she croaked.

Alison raised her drooping head from the table and pushed her untidy hair out of her eyes.

"Oh, Granny, Master Nowell was on and on at me to say you were a witch, and Mistress Chattox and Anne. I kept saying it wasn't true but he wouldn't believe me – he means to hang us all."

Atterlothe said, "The course is set. Now we must try to steer it as best we can."

The Silver Hare raised its head. "And how do you intend to do that?"

The Elven King replied, "At this moment Alison Demdike is denouncing Old Demdike and the Chattoxes for all she is worth. She has changed her tune and is singing like a blackbird in Spring. The song she sings is of black arts, poppets, familiars, bewitchings and murders. She confesses readily to all. The second oldest Demdike is nothing if not inventive. I suspect she is enjoying herself enormously. Indeed, she goes so far that I wonder how an educated man like Nowell can swallow it all."

Mistress Demdike leaped to her feet in a rage.

"The second oldest Demdike means to destroy us all! You must stop her Atterlothe. Have you taken leave of your senses?"

The Chovihani laid a restraining hand on her arm.

"Be calm, Mistress. You have not yet grasped our plan. It is better for us to control who is denounced, and when. In this way we can have the puppets ready, the Spirits of the Dead inside them to play their part. Far better for the puppets to be arrested than be forced to effect a dangerous rescue."

Light began to dawn on Old Demdike's wrinkled face. "Hmm," she sounded grudging, and the children remembered that she would be the only one who would have to play the part of herself.

Atterlothe spoke gently. "It is best this way. Tonight Mistress Chattox and Anne will come with us to the Faery

Realms where you will be safe. The Spirits of the Dead inside your puppets shall take your place."

That which all had been expecting vaguely for many months had come upon them with a horrible reality. Old Demdike spoke in a shaky voice with none of her usual swagger.

"It is all up with me then. I go to hold the Glamour and I go to my death."

"Not necessarily," said Aunt Salome. "I have given this problem much attention. I will say no more for now. Do that which you know you must – hold the Glamour, play your part well and I believe you will live to kick up your heels at the Autumn Equinox along with the best of us."

A gleam of hope shone in the eyes of Mistress Demdike. "What is your plan?"

But The Chovihani refused to be drawn. "It will unfold," was all she would say, and with that, Old Demdike was forced to be content.

17. A Strange Feast

Three days later, the village of Barley was agog with the news that Old Demdike and the Chattox Family had been arrested and taken by Master Nowell to the home of his friend James Wilsey, a fellow magistrate who lived in the settlement of Fence, along with Alison. It was the most exciting thing that had happened in the district for many a long year and gossip spread like wildfire.

"Sold their souls to the Devil himself, so they do say."

"A black dog for a familiar, eyes as red as coals and the size of a horse."

"Boiling up dead babies to use the fat in their wicked spells. My Harry did see them and they did strike him dead."

In the Smith's cottage, Jennet was distraught. She seemed to have lost weight over the last few days and appeared smaller and skinnier than ever.

"Jennet," Ma said sternly, as they sat at supper one evening, "You must eat. Look at you, a parcel of bones."

"I keep thinking of Granny and the terrible things people are saying about her, and my food won't go down. What if Aunt Salome's plan doesn't work?"

Ma tried to console her as best she could. When Atterlothe appeared later that evening, Jennet was still huddled miserably by the fire.

"This thing needs to be moved on," he said. "The Glamour cannot be held forever and we should get Jennet and Jimmy away from here. We must precipitate the last of the arrests. I propose a party should be held at Malkin Tower. Good Friday is a day or so away - that will shock the Vicar - a witch's party on a Christian feast day."

"A party?" Ma was intrigued.

"Yes. Those who have not yet been arrested shall be there drawing attention to themselves by…"

"Stealing a sheep?" Jimmy piped up. "My Jimmy steal a sheep," he said. He always referred to himself as 'my Jimmy'.

"Steal it for the witches' party. My Jimmy make sure he is caught – lead them to Malkin Tower."

He so rarely spoke that it took them by surprise.

"Well done, Jimmy," said Wayland Smith, "that should work well. I imagine the puppets will be ready at Malkin Tower, but who will hold the Glamour? Mistress Demdike will not be there."

"I will," said Emmet.

There was a shocked silence.

"You, Emmet?" said the Elven King. "Are you sure? This is no light matter."

Emmet, with all eyes on him, blushed and said, "I want to help. I want to do something for Jennet. I've been practising night after night with Pooka. I am one of the Chosen. I am ready. Please let me do it."

The star shone out of his forehead. Mistress Smith's eyes filled with tears of pride and concern. Jennet reached out and touched his foot. The familiar pink glow surrounded them both, lighting up the cottage.

"Thank you, Emmet."

That night as they went to bed, Hetty and Letty whispered together under the bedclothes.

"Do you think it's fair," Letty grumbled, "for Emmet to do exciting things on his own all the time?" Hetty didn't. "Let's help him."

"And me!" Lily sat up in bed. "I'm coming too."

The twins had thought she was asleep. "No, Lily, you're too little."

"Am not," said Lily with injured dignity. "Who knocked out Roger Nowell, anyway? If you don't let me come, I'll tell Ma."

"I'm coming as well." Jennet's voice sounded from the bed along the wall. "It's my family, after all."

Saffron fluttered out of her sheep's wool bed and settled cross-legged on the gay patchwork quilt.

"You are all naughty, every one of you. I'd better come, too, then. You may need me."

157

On the morning of Good Friday, Jimmy noisily and clumsily stole a sheep and dragged it by a string, baa-ing indignantly all the way to Malkin Tower where Atterlothe was waiting with the puppets. Elizabeth Demdike was animated by the oldest Old Demdike, Jennet by the youngest Old Demdike, Jimmy by Billy and Mistress Alice Nutter by the spirit of Old Mrs. Law. An extraordinary sight to behold.

"I won't have to say much, will I?" Billy asked. "I'm afraid of getting it wrong. I don't want to get Jimmy into trouble."

Jimmy grinned at his double. "My Jimmy in trouble already. Nothing my Billy can say make it worse."

"Do not fear," said the Oldest Demdike. "Concentrate on animating the puppet. I will speak for you."

The Mistress Alice puppet wandered around the filthy hovel picking things up and putting them down again, aimlessly.

"Don't reckon much to having a body again. There's a lot to be said for being dead."

The Elizabeth Demdike puppet replied, "Oh I don't know. A body that is neither human nor faery, cannot die and needs no food. If taken care of, it could last forever. What say you sister?"

The Jennet puppet simpered, "Why do you think I chose the youngest and sweetest?"

Old Mrs. Law snorted. "Foolish talk. I for one shall be glad to be back in my comfortable grave. My babies will be missing me."

Emmet, in the shape of a hare, arrived outside the hovel. It was the first time in the realm of men that he had changed by himself, and it had gone well. He studied Malkin Tower. It was a blot on the landscape, broken windows stuffed with rags, the door hanging off its hinges, part of a derelict farmhouse which seemed at one time to have been half burned down. No wonder Jennet and Jimmy had not wanted the Smith children to see where they lived.

He slipped in through the broken door and Changed, greeted by Atterlothe and Jimmy. The puppets were seated around a woodworm-ridden table. If they had appeared real before, now they were animated by the Spirits of the Dead it was impossible to tell that they were not truly alive. The Jennet puppet spoke first.

"Welcome, my True Lover. Come and give your sweetheart a kiss. Don't be shy."

Emmet recoiled in horror. The voice, the face were Jennet's, but the words and the brazen way in which they were spoken were so unlike modest Jennet that his skin crawled.

"That's enough!" Atterlothe was shaken out of his normal mild manner.

"Just a bit of fun," the Jennet puppet pouted. "I mean nothing, just amusing myself."

"Can you manage the Glamour, Emmet?" asked the Elven King. "I am holding it for now. You will only need to do so until they are arrested, which will happen fairly soon. The Old Ones themselves can hold it until they are with Mistress Demdike."

"Of course," Emmet said, trying to sound confident. "Don't worry, Atterlothe."

Meanwhile, Jimmy had been looking out from the half-opened door. "Farmer and Master Nowell's constable are coming. No time for My Jimmy to escape now. My Jimmy and Emmet hide in loft."

He pointed to a broken loft ladder and he and Emmet scrambled up it as fast as they could. Atterlothe gave the puppets a last, troubled look before vanishing so that the universe barely flickered. Emmet and Jimmy sat silently in the loft space, waiting. They could see the farmer and the constable out of a broken part of the roof, a few minutes away across the fields. The Farmer was gesticulating angrily to the constable who walked stolidly along at his side.

Back at the forge, the girls had set off together towards the forest, ostensibly to collect kindling for the forge. This was a task that none of them were fond of, and if Ma had not been distracted by anxiety about Emmet and The Glamour, her suspicions might have been aroused. As it was, she waved them off vaguely and returned to her worrying. Once hidden among the trees, Jennet put down her basket.

"We need to get to Malkin Tower as swiftly as we can. Should we go as hares?"

"Not fast enough," said Letty. "It's almost the middle of the morning." She glanced at her sister who grinned excitedly.

"We thought we could fly."

Lily was enchanted. "I love flying!"

Jennet was more cautious.

"We've only done it with Savine watching us in the Faery Realms. Do you think we could do it here, alone? We'd have to be invisible as well. If anyone saw us …"

"We can do it." Hetty and Letty said, as one. "We thought we would use the wood baskets as we didn't bring broomsticks."

Four wood baskets were soon flying over the treetops towards Malkin Tower. Saffron had prudently put herself in charge of keeping them all invisible, casting a double spell which made them visible to each other.

"So that we don't lose each other," she explained.

Jennet led the way, Lily next with Saffron and the twins holding hands side by side behind them.

Lily looked down nervously over the forest. "We've never flown so high before," she said.

"Don't be afraid, Lily," said Saffron, "we are nearly there."

Sure enough, the burned and blackened roof of Malkin Tower was close now. Jennet squinted down over the edge of her basket.

"Oh dear, there is the farmer with Roger Nowell's constable. We are late."

"We've still got time," said Saffron. "They've got to walk right across that field. Where is a good place to land, Jennet?"

"On the roof – look, can you see where that big hole is? We can climb through it and drag the baskets after us. The loft is underneath. We can put them there while we…" Her voice trailed off uncertainly.

"While we what?" asked Lily.

"Well, whatever we do next. Hetty and Letty, what *do* we do next?"

Silence from the last two baskets.

"Haven't we got a plan?" asked Jennet.

"Not exactly," they admitted, reluctantly. "We thought you had one."

"It was your idea," Jennet said, exasperated. "Have you brought us here using dangerous magic just to…"

What she would have said, they never knew, for just then, Lily let out a piercing shriek. "Jennet, look out!"

Jennet spun round but it was too late. Her lapse in concentration had caused the flying spell to falter and the baskets whirled out of control, lurching crazily downwards towards the tower.

"Hold on tight!" screamed Saffron, rather unnecessarily, as they plummeted through the air. She hurled a handful of faery dust and uttered a short charm. A split second before they hit the roof, the baskets slowed, rolling gently through the hole in it and spilling their terrified occupants on top of Emmet and Jimmy. Saffron threw another pinch of faery dust and everyone became visible again, struggling to get upright.

"Sorry Emmet, sorry Jimmy. Are you alright?"

Emmet was aghast. "What are you doing here? The constable will come through that door any second. If he sees you here, everything will be ruined. Roger Nowell will find out about the puppets and everyone will be arrested – Ma and Pa included."

Hetty and Letty hung their heads in shame while Jennet's voice wobbled.

"We're sorry, Emmet, we wanted to help. We didn't properly think it through. We'll go back to the Forge, shall we? We truly are sorry."

A querulous voice called up the ladder.

"What's going on up there? The constable is coming up

161

the path. Stop that racket and concentrate on holding the Glamour. Must we do everything? It's easy enough to hold when we are still, but not when we are talking, and I think we may have to do quite a bit of that shortly."

Saffron took charge of what was threatening to become a lost cause.

"Listen to me, everyone. Sit in a circle and hold hands. Don't say a word. Focus on the Glamour – oh, wait, the ladder! We don't want the constable up here."

She threw more faery dust and the ladder shot up through the hole, hanging itself neatly on a cracked beam.

"Alright down there," she called softly. "We have it all under control. Just play your part."

"I just hope you have, that's all – constable, this is private property. What do you mean by bursting into our home like this?"

These last words were shrieked loudly to let Emmet know that the men had arrived. Saffron hissed under her breath with great urgency, "The Glamour. Empty your minds of everything else. On the count of three."

In the event, Emmet was relieved to have the unexpected help of others. Holding the Glamour was the most difficult thing he could have imagined. For whole moments at a time he would feel he had it, then it would slip through a crack in his mind to be grasped in the nick of time by Jimmy, or even Lily, and held until they too lost it and it was seized by someone else. Downstairs, confused shouting continued.

"We'll blow up Lancaster Gaol, that's what we'll do."

"That's my sheep officer. I told you that young ruffian had it. Take him into custody."

"Can't a family have a meal without the law upsetting everything?"

"We are having a feast and making clay poppets, that is what we are doing. Do you want to see the human teeth we have, Master Hargreaves? Granny got them from the graveyard, so she did."

"Silence!" The voice of Henry Hargreaves boomed out

across the babble, unable to get a word in edgeways. "I have heard enough. Blowing up Lancaster Gaol? I only came to see about the sheep, so I did. Making poppets? You've condemned yourselves out of your own mouths. Master Nowell will want to question you about this, no mistake. It'll be Gallows Hill for you, I wouldn't wonder. And you, Mistress Nutter, mixed up with these fiends of hell in this filthy hovel – if I had not seen it with my own two eyes I never would have credited it. I'm arresting the whole lot of you. Farmer, help me tie their hands. And don't turn your back on any of 'em for an instant."

"We'll not speak again until we are before the magistrate," came the voice of the Oldest Old Demdike. "I say, *we'll not speak again until we are before the magistrate*."

"We can let go," whispered Saffron. "She is letting us know that they can manage now."

"No need to shout," said Henry Hargreaves, indignantly. "I heard you the first time. Save it for Master Nowell."

There was a scuffling down below as the prisoners were tied up and led away across the fields.

18. A TROUBLING DISCOVERY

Emmet heaved a huge sigh, breaking the silence that followed. Sweat was pouring down his face. He felt sick and dizzy. Jimmy peered at him with a look of concern.

"Get my Emmet water... rest now."

He put the ladder back in place and scuttled down, returning with a dirty flagon of water which he offered to Emmet. Saffron took a tiny phial from the pocket she had hanging from her waist and put a few drops of Liquid Life Force into the flagon. "We should all have some," she said. They did, and colour returned to their faces.

"That was so hard," said Emmet. "I'm glad now that you came, I couldn't have done it on my own."

The girls were relieved, but Jennet leaned forward and rested her chin on her knees, still anxious.

"What is it, Jennet?"

"There was something not right. It shouldn't have been so hard. I mean, it is a difficult thing to hold but there were seven of us all working as hard as we could. I felt almost... no, that can't be right."

"Go on." Saffron was listening intently.

"Well, I felt as though something was working against us."

"Or someone." There was a grim look on Saffron's tiny face.

"Who would want to work against us?" said Emmet. "I thought everyone wanted to help. The Old Ones said they were doing it for True Love," he added, turning pink and avoiding Jennet's eye.

Jennet blushed too. She said, "I don't trust them. Remember how horrid they were to Granny in the graveyard, how they laughed when no one would play her part? They are up to something, I know they are. I just wish we knew what."

"We must talk to Atterlothe," said Saffron. "The plan has worked so far. Now we should go home. Are we going to fly?"

There was an anxious silence.

"I don't think we can," said Hetty and Letty together. "We don't feel so good."

Jennet agreed. "I don't feel so good either. Even after the Liquid Life Force, I don't think I could cast a spell to save my life."

"We should use our Silver Hares," said Lily, always surprising them. "Don't you remember? The Silver Hare said that in times of trouble, we only had to ask and they would bring us home."

"Oh, well remembered, Lily."

Emmet gave his sister a hug.

"Does this count as being in times of trouble, do you think?" Lily asked.

"If this isn't trouble, I don't know what is," said Saffron, tartly. "We can't walk home. Jennet and Jimmy have been arrested, or so the constable thinks. If anyone should see them walking through the forest, well!"

"How does it work?" asked Emmet pulling the amulet out from under his shirt, tied to a length of string.

"Hold it in your hand and say, 'Please take me home'," explained Saffron. "Remember to say please - the universe does like to be asked nicely."

They all took out their Silver Hares and did a splendid countdown from three to one, then, "Please take me home" they chorused. The universe, on cue, shuddered and turned itself inside out. They had the curious sensation of being sucked through a whirling tunnel lit by bright lights. Lily opened her mouth to scream, but before she could utter a sound the universe righted itself neatly, depositing them all in a tangle of arms and legs on the floor of the cottage, the wood baskets, neatly stacked, arriving a second later.

Ma and Pa, sitting one on either side of the fireplace supping mugs of mead, gaped at the writhing pile of children.

19. A Disturbing Discovery

Atterlothe slipped into the cottage late that evening where the children and Saffron poured out everything that had happened at Malkin Tower. The Elven King was troubled by their difficulty in holding the Glamour and by the idea of a force working against them.

"I do not know what to make of this," he said. "The Old Ones are not of our company nor bound by our rigorous code of goodness. In life they trod a dark path and the ends they met were not pleasant. They were burned to death by an angry mob that took the law into its own hands. They barricaded themselves into their home to escape, but the people set the house on fire. Only one person escaped, the youngest Old Demdike's daughter. The story goes that the child gave them away to save herself, but I don't know the truth."

"Where did they live?" asked Jennet, suspecting the answer.

Atterlothe did not look at her. "In Malkin Tower."

Emmet thought of the burned and blackened appearance of the Demdike family home and his scalp prickled with horror.

"It was a long time ago," said Atterlothe, trying to lighten the atmosphere. "Two hundred years in human terms. No one in the Pendle area remembers it."

"My Granny is ancient," Jennet said. "Could she be two hundred years old?"

Mistress Smith exchanged looks with Pa and Atterlothe.

"It is unlikely," she said, "but not impossible. She has much knowledge, that is certain."

"What if she was that girl?" suggested Jennet. "What if this is the Old Ones' chance for revenge?"

Jimmy looked up at Atterlothe. "What name of girl?"

Atterlothe cleared his throat uneasily. He did not want to speak the name, but he had to.

"Jennet," he said. "Jennet Demdike."

Jennet looked devastated. "That's my Granny's name. I was named after her. She was that girl, I know she was. That's what Granny meant when she said our blood was tainted. Oh Atterlothe, whatever do they mean to do to her?"

Mistress Smith put her arms around the weeping girl.

"I do not know, sweetheart," she said, "but what I do know is that your Granny is prepared to sacrifice herself for you and for the Company of the Silver Hare. Everyone in Barley will know that you and Jimmy were arrested at Malkin Tower. You cannot remain here. Your Ma and Mistress Alice have already gone to the Faery Realms. You must go now, this minute. The gossips will be knocking on our door to find out what we know. They cannot find you here. If they do, all our plans will come to naught and our family, my children, will be in peril."

Jennet stared at her wildly through her tears. "We can't leave Granny."

Wayland Smith took her hand. "Don't forget that Aunt Salome has a plan. If anyone can save Old Demdike, The Chovihani can."

A loud knocking on the cottage door ended their secret talk. Everyone froze, the knocking sounded again, and a voice called from outside.

"Mistress Smith, Mistress Smith, be you abed? Open this door, I beg you. I bear tidings you'll be wanting to hear and no mistake. Open up, for pity's sake."

Wayland Smith moved swiftly to the connecting door that led to the forge, opened it and motioned them silently to leave. Atterlothe grabbed Jimmy and Jennet, drawing them into the dark forge. Wayland Smith closed it softly behind them and shot the bolts.

Atterlothe took out a wand and held it up. A blue flame shone from the tip. In its light he found the silver horseshoe which he stood on its prongs. He threw a pinch of faery dust and uttered the charm. The last thing Jennet and Jimmy heard as Atterlothe led them through the archway was the sound of Ma's voice.

"Mercy, Mistress Hewitt, what can you have to tell me at this time of night? I hope it's good news – we are about to go to our beds. Come in, come in. You are letting out good heat."

20. A SURPRISING VISITOR

It was a trying time for the Smith family. Everyone in the village knew that Jimmy and Jennet had lived with them, and people were constantly knocking on the door hoping for tales of witchcraft, spells and curses. Mistress Smith patiently repeated that she had seen no evidence of any such thing, but this was not what the village wanted to hear. The good folk of Barley seemed to have completely forgotten that Jimmy and Jennet were kind and helpful young people of whom they themselves had been rather fond. As for Mistress Alice, there were many who rather enjoyed the fact that the lady of the manor had fallen from grace. Ma forbade Emmet from visiting the Faery Realms for the time being.

"I know it is hard, son, but we cannot risk any use of magic whatsoever. The eyes of Pendle are watching for us to make one false step. We must give absolutely nothing away."

Emmet was deeply upset. He had had no opportunity to say good-bye to Jennet or Pooka. He assumed he would be able to visit them every day in the Faery Realms. As time passed, he missed Jennet more than he could have believed possible. It felt as though a piece of his heart had been stolen and left him with a cold, hollow feeling. Saffron, who stubbornly remained on her windowsill, was the only contact with the Faery Realms which they had, and although she brought messages from time to time, it was not the same.

"The worst thing," said Hetty one morning when the girls had just woken up, "is feeling ordinary. I'm beginning to feel ordinary again."

"Sometimes," Letty agreed, "I wonder if we ever did magic or met Speedwell or flew or did any of those things. It's only been a few weeks, but sometimes I wonder if it was all a dream."

Lily spoke from Jennet's bed, which she had taken to sleeping in as none of them could bear to see it empty.

"When Jimmy and Jennet were here," she said wistfully,

"I was beginning to feel big. Now they've gone, I feel small again."

Hetty and Letty couldn't help laughing at that.

"Oh Lily, come in our bed and have a cuddle."

Midsummer passed, but the children didn't enjoy the fire on Pendle Hill, although Ma insisted that they all went as usual to keep up appearances. Nor did they visit the older children in the graveyard.

"It's been a year," said Emmet sadly, "a year yesterday since we got to know Jennet and Jimmy, and a year today since the special egg hatched and it all began. How much longer must we be ordinary, Ma? I'm one of the Chosen; I need to be learning more things with Pooka."

Ma patted his cheek. "When it's all over. It won't be long now. After Lammas tide, Aunt Salome said. Do you remember?"

A few more weeks dragged on. The prisoners were held at Lancaster Gaol and nothing had been heard of them apart from the fact that they were awaiting trial. The initial excitement in the village had died down and the villagers were busy in field and garden. Emmet and the girls tried to settle down to their old existence until one night something happened which changed everything.

It was the night of the new moon, dark and overcast, with no stars showing. The Smith Family were just about to retire to their beds when the candles in the cottage guttered and went out. A feeling of deathly cold swept through the room. There was a strong graveyard smell permeating the atmosphere.

"Who's there?" called out Pa, sharply. "Show yourself."

A pale light began to form, and the familiar wispy spirit of old Mrs. Law appeared before them.

"Mrs. Law, whatever are you doing here? Why are you not in the castle?"

The spirit wrung its ghostly hands in agitation.

"Oh, Mistress Smith, Master Smith, you must come and help. It's Mistress Demdike. She be in a bad way. She be near death, I think."

"Calm down, Mrs. Law," said Pa, "try to tell us what is happening. Take your time."

"I haven't got much time, Master, and that's a fact. I told the Old Ones I was just nipping back to the graveyard to visit my babes. The Truth is, The Old Ones are up to no good, and Old Mistress Demdike she can't hardly hold the Glamour no more. I don't know what the Old Ones be about, but it be like they are sucking the life out of her. And young Billy, he be so scared of them, his spirit has gone home."

"Gone home?" Ma was horrified. "But how will the Jimmy puppet stand trial if Billy has gone?"

"I don't know Mistress, I'm sure. At present the guards just think he is ill. The puppet don't do nothing, you see, just sits there. But there's worse. The Jennet puppet, she ain't in the gaol at all. That youngest Old Demdike, she accused all the others, left, right and centre of terrible things, doings what a body's imagination couldn't never dream up. Now she ain't on trial at all, she's a witness for the prosecution. Where she be, I don't rightly know; in the magistrate's house perhaps."

"This is bad," Pa said. "Mistress Law, it is kind of you to come here. You did the right thing. Go back to your puppet now. We will talk to the Silver Hare. Tell Mistress Demdike that help is on its way. Tell her to hold on. Be discreet," he added quickly, "try not to let the Old Ones hear you."

Old Mrs. Law bobbed a ghostly curtsey and vanished, along with the graveyard smell and icy chill.

"We must speak to Atterlothe," said Wayland Smith. "The Old Ones are out of control. I do not understand what they are doing. Saffron, please, will you fetch him for us?"

In a trice, with a shudder of the Universe, Atterlothe, the Chovihani and the Silver Hare all appeared. Ma quickly cast a circle and set repelling charms all around the cottage.

"So," the Silver Hare spoke in its starry voice, "the Old Ones work for their own dark ends. My Sister," it inclined its head to the Chovihani, "Will you scry for us again? Wayland, your breast plate, if you please."

Pa fetched it from the forge and set it carefully on the kitchen table. Ma emptied a jug of Holy Well water into it and Henny Penny hopped out of the basket by the fire and pulled out one of her long tail feathers. She was looking sad and bedraggled since Jimmy had gone, her usually sleek feathers sticking out in all directions. Candles were lit, Aunt Salome stroked the surface of the water with the feather and once again a silvery mist rose from the bowl. The old Egyptian peered into it and snapped her fingers.

"It has changed," she said, abruptly. "I see the hanged figures, and Old Demdike and Jennet are not amongst them. The Old Ones have altered the future."

"But surely that's a good thing, isn't it?" asked Letty, puzzled.

"Not exactly," said Aunt Salome. "We have sought to change the meaning of the future. That is one thing. The Old Ones have changed the future itself."

The children tried to understand but didn't see the difference.

"I think," said The Chovihani, "that it is time to put my plan into action. Someone must visit old Demdike in prison. Visitors are allowed. We take a powerful potion to give Old Demdike just before the hanging. There is a tradition of allowing prisoners to stop at the tavern on the way to Gallows Hill for a final drink with their friends and family. The potion would make her appear to collapse and die. No one would have been surprised, such an old woman under so much strain. It would have saved the hangman a job. The prisoners are taken from the Gaol in a cart with their coffins so that their relatives can bring them home for burial. We would have put her in her coffin and revived her later. It would have worked. But now we cannot wait for the trial. Old Demdike must appear to die as soon as possible."

Atterlothe said, "How will that be accomplished? In human terms, it is a long ride to Lancaster. We might be too late to save her."

"Aunt Salome," said Wayland, "once the potion is

172

administered, how long before she must be revived?"

"As long as you like, years if necessary. She will be in a state of suspended animation. But," she added, "she must still be alive when you give it to her, of course."

"Very well. Saffron, will you take the potion to her now? Tell her what it is, and that Mistress Smith and I will come and take her body home. Tell her to have no fear, we will revive her as soon as we can. Aunt Salome?"

The Chovihani took out a small bottle. "Three drops will be enough. No more and no less."

Saffron reached out a tiny hand.

"Are you happy to do this?" asked Wayland Smith. "It is a great imposition, I know."

"No one will see me," said Saffron. "I shall be back in no time. I am so small, it is best that I go. Don't worry."

She snapped her fingers and vanished, with the Universe giving a tiny ripple.

"Tomorrow," said Ma, "we shall take care to let the whole village know we are going. We will visit the Vicar and the neighbours and say that our Christian consciences dictate that we take food and medicine to the prisoners, the fallen unfortunates of our parish. We will ask if anyone would like to contribute. They will consider us foolish but saintly. In this way, when we return with Mistress Demdike in her coffin, no one will be surprised. And with Wayland as the new grave digger, all will be well."

Atterlothe was still concerned, and said, "When we have rescued Mistress Demdike, there will only be the Old Ones to hold the Glamour. This worries me. I do not know what their plan is, but the stars speak of a great evil. The Wild Hunt was low in the sky last night. My Lord, I am greatly uneasy."

21. TOO LATE

The Universe gave an almost imperceptible shiver, and Saffron appeared before them on the table,

"I was too late," she said, in stricken tones. "Mistress Demdike breathed her last before I could give her the potion."

There was a stunned silence. Emmet felt a cold hand clutch at his stomach. The Chovihani was the first to recover.

"So, the puppets are beyond our control, and Mistress Demdike has met the fate she feared. I do not know what more can be done." She shrugged her shoulders as though throwing off the whole affair.

"Perhaps," Emmet spoke tentatively, "now they're revenged on Old Demdike, they'll see the plan through. They did seem to want to help Jennet. She is their great-granddaughter after all, and she hasn't done anything wrong."

"I hope for all our sakes that you are right," said the Elven King. "I cannot see what they could have to gain by exposing the puppets for what they are. It is easy enough to move the Smiths to the safety of the Faery Realms, but it would start a witch-hunt in England the like of which has never been seen. No follower of the Great Mother would be safe the length and breadth of the land should such magic be discovered. It would almost have been better," he added bitterly, "not to interfere and let our beloved Company die."

The Silver Hare touched Atterlothe gently with its paw.

"Where light shines," it said, "darkness cannot long hold sway. We have done what we have done in good faith and with stout hearts. One sister stepped from the path of light and has paid the price. But she has died a hero's death trying to right her wrong. All is not over." It turned its shining head to Ma. "My dear, continue with your original plan and bring us back the body of our fallen sister."

The next day saw the Smith Family departing by horse and cart for Lancaster castle. As Ma had predicted, the vicar thought them foolish but good hearted, and a few of the villagers contributed small comforts. It was a long and bumpy ride, with frequent stops to ford streams and even to push when the going got particularly rough. It was late that night when they wearily trundled into Lancaster. Pa and Emmet slept the night on sheepskins in the back of the cart whilst Ma and the girls shared a bed in one of the many inns.

The children had never visited a town before and were astounded by the noise, smells, hustle and bustle. Lily especially was daunted by it all. As they wended their way to the castle, she clung tightly to Emmet's hand, but the twins were enchanted and kept running off to look at the sights. Ma became exasperated with them.

"Stay with us, for pity's sake. The last thing we need now is for one of you to get lost. We are on a serious errand so please try to remember that. Get back in the cart."

When they reached the castle, Pa announced that he was going in alone.

"There will be sights in there that I don't want you young'uns to see. Stay here with Ma. I will be as quick as I can."

Mistress Smith and the girls sat in the back of the cart whilst Emmet talked to the old horse and stroked its nose. It was wonderful being able to understand the speech of animals, and the old creature was in the middle of a long and involved story about a distant cousin when Pa returned, his face pale and set.

"Bring the cart up to the main gate, Emmet," he said, abruptly.

Emmet obeyed. Shortly, two rough looking men emerged with a crude wooden coffin and heaved it carelessly onto the cart.

"Cheated the hangman she did," observed one, dusting off his grimy hands.

"Aye," said his friend, "that's one old hag who's cursed her last."

He spat on the coffin then held out his hand expectantly

to Wayland Smith. Pa eyed him with distaste but handed him a couple of coins.

"A drink for your trouble. Good day to you both."

It was a weary, dispirited family that bore the body of Mistress Demdike back to the village of Barley. The vicar made it clear that he would have nothing to do with the burial.

"She did not live or die as a Christian should and I will not bury her as such. She should count herself lucky to be in the graveyard at all. I've half a mind to put her under the high road with a stake through her heart along with the suicides."

Ma murmured that this might cause Old Demdike to haunt the Vicar who turned pale at the thought.

"The churchyard, then," he said hastily, "but bury her on the north side with the unbaptised babies."

Pa clicked to the old horse, trundling the cart with its gruesome burden back to the forge. He and Emmet carried the coffin inside and set it down between two stools. Ma announced that she would see to the laying out of the body herself, something she often did for the old folk of the village.

Hetty and Letty came to an unspoken agreement.

"Ma, please can we help you?" asked Letty.

"If Jennet was here," added Hetty, "we know that she would want to, and as she isn't, we thought we could do it for her."

Ma stared at them in surprise then drew her daughters to her for a hug.

"That is a kind thought. I'm proud of you both and I'm sure that Jennet will be grateful when she knows. It is something you should learn to do in any case."

That night, Pa lit up the forge with candles and lifted the body of Old Demdike onto the table which had been covered with a sheet. Ma brought bowls of warm water scented with sweet herbs, cloths and towels, and a clean linen winding sheet. Hetty and Letty stood beside her rather nervously. Ma called in the four directions and cast a circle as Pa retreated into the cottage with Emmet and Lily.

"First of all," Mistress Smith explained, "we shall give her a good wash, then dress her in the winding sheet and do her hair. I have sweet strewing herbs to line the coffin, then Pa shall lay her in it for us."

They began to undress the shrivelled body of Old Mistress Demdike. Ma carefully closed her eyes, which in death appeared to glare horribly, whilst her lips were drawn back from her toothless gums in a fierce grin that was rather unnerving. She was thin and light, making the unpleasant job of removing her clothes easier than might have been, but she seemed to be wearing layer upon layer of filthy, appallingly smelly rags. The twins felt sick but persevered bravely. They had almost got down to her tattered chemise when Letty found the old woman's amulet, worn around her neck on a fine gold chain. Strung next to it was a tiny bottle covered with intricate metal work of exotic design.

"Look at this." She held it up to the candlelight. "It has something in it."

She was about to pull out the stopper when Ma quickly took it from her.

"Don't uncork it!" They stopped and waited for Ma to explain. "I know what it is. It's a liquid letter. The faery folk often use them, and so do members of our Company. You pour the liquid onto a piece of cloth or parchment, say the visibility charm and a letter will appear. It stops information falling into the wrong hands."

"But if somebody sent her a liquid letter," said Hetty, puzzled, "why didn't she read it?"

"I don't think anyone sent it to her," Ma said. "I believe she wrote it herself. It is a message for the Company. She hoped, as has happened, that we would retrieve her body."

So saying, she removed it carefully from the chain and put it in the bosom of her gown.

Old Demdike was so filthy that the laying out took time, but at last she was wrapped in the spotless winding sheet, smelling of attar of roses. Her hair, which they had always assumed was grey, turned out after washing to be a beautiful snowy white. Hetty braided it neatly and wrapped it around the wizened head. When all was done, they stood back to pay their respects.

"Poor Mistress Demdike," Letty shook her head sadly, "why did she let herself get so dirty? Jennet and Alison and Jimmy aren't like that."

Ma put an arm around each twin.

"Perhaps," she said soberly, "when you have a stain on your soul, it becomes harder to keep your body clean."

Mistress Demdike was buried the next day on the north side of the graveyard. No one from the village attended. Wayland Smith and Emmet lowered the coffin into the deep hole that Pa had dug. Ma said a prayer to the Great Mother and they all sang a hymn. Pa filled in the grave and Lily planted a rose bush, dug up from Ma's garden.

"I thought at least the Spirits of the Dead might have come," said Emmet. "It seems odd that no one from the Company came. I thought at least Atterlothe or Aunt Salome might have been here."

"When someone dies," explained Pa, "it takes a while for their spirit to detach from their body. We won't see anything of old Demdike now until All Souls Night. Then the Spirits will have a welcoming party for her. That is why there is no one else here. The Faery Folk just fade so they do not have funerals, and the Egyptians burn their dead in their carts or tents."

"I am glad," said Lily. "I thought Mistress Demdike's friends were being horrid, but I didn't like to say anything. I couldn't understand why we hadn't seen her spirit. I thought she wasn't speaking to us because we washed her."

Ma went into a peal of sudden laughter

"Oh Lily, you are so funny sometimes!"

22. MESSAGE IN A BOTTLE

That night, Atterlothe, The Chovihani and The Silver Hare materialized in the forge. Ma presented the hare with the bottle taken from Old Demdike's body.

"Have you a handkerchief, Mistress Smith?"

Ma had a clean one ready and laid it on the table. The Silver Hare removed the stopper, poured the contents onto the white fabric and uttered a charm. Letters began to appear, wobbly and jumbled at first, but quickly sorting themselves into this message:

To the Company of the Silver Hare,

If this letter comes into your possession, as I hope and pray it will, then I shall have died in this terrible place.

What I write to you now is both a confession and a warning.

I am over two hundred years old and I am both weary of life but at the same time afraid to die.

I am the daughter of the youngest Old Demdike. As a child I was brought up by the three of them in Malkin Tower. The most corrupt and evil witches, they were – are – more foul than anyone could imagine. They taught me their evil ways, at the same time ill-treating me mercilessly. I hated and feared them and longed to be an ordinary child in an ordinary home.

When I was nine years old, they went too far. They were trying to make the elixir of life, for which a great many innocent babes died mysteriously.

I betrayed them to the villagers and a mob came in the night setting fire to the tower. They died cursing the name of Jennet Demdike.

No one in the village would take in the witch's brat and I lived in the part of the tower that escaped the fire, fending for myself as best I could in Pendle Forest.

When I grew to womanhood, I earned my living as a cunning woman with my herbs and potions. I staved off old age

179

with spells, and the elixir which the Old Ones had made. For a hundred and fifty years I looked no older than a woman of thirty. I cloaked myself in charms of forgetfulness so that Pendle would not remember my age or where I came from. I was terrified of death. I knew the Old Ones were waiting for me on the other side and would torture my spirit for evermore. I tried only to tread the path of light and joined the Company of the Silver Hare. My daughter was born, and later my grandchildren, but the darkness caught up with me, a curse here, a poppet there. The strain of living in the light was too hard. I, who was raised in darkness, could no longer bear the light. Old age came creeping at my door as I ran out of elixir. I would not kill a child to replace it. I was a grey witch, not a black one. My daughter is grey also, and any stain on her soul is my doing and my regret, but my grandchildren tread only in the light. My Alison, my Jimmy, Jennet my namesake, my Scarlet Flower, pure as the Jennet I would like to have been.

I have led the Company into trouble, that I freely admit, although with lack of care, not malice. The Silver Hare, who sees all things, knows that to be the truth. I had hoped, by holding the Glamour, to save the Company, and I was foolish enough to believe that the Old Ones would play their part for their great-granddaughter and for True Love. I knew that I would likely die in this enterprise but I was glad to make the sacrifice for those I love, although I am sore afraid of eternity with the Old Ones.

I underestimated them. At first, I could not understand what was wrong. I could not hold the Glamour. Every attempt left me weaker, despite dosing myself continuously with Liquid Life Force. I felt as though they were working against me, yet at the same time, the Glamour seemed to be holding itself. The puppets have become more real with every day that passes. At night, here in this wretched prison, the other spirits leave the puppets to rest. Not so the Old Ones. They never leave the puppets they inhabit.

Tonight, as close to death as I am, the truth has come to me. The Old Demdike Sisters will not return to their graveyard *when all here is over. They want to live forever. We have played into their wicked hands. We have given them bodies for their spirits to live in, bodies which can never age, which if treated carefully will never wear out.*

The Jennet Puppet – the Youngest Old Demdike – my mother, curse her rotten soul, has denounced all the others so vilely to even shock the men of law. She will escape and the rest will hang. You must find her and destroy her. This will be the hardest task for she has great cunning and power.

Wayland Smith, my good friend, after the hangings you must be sure not to leave the puppets for a moment until you cut them down and burn them. Remember, they <u>must</u> be burned. No other method of destruction will do. I would rather my spirit suffer eternal torture at the hands of theirs than see this terrible evil let loose on an unsuspecting world.

I grow weary. My end is close and for now at least, I am not sorry.

I embrace you all, my good friends.
Mistress Jennet Demdike

There was a deathly silence broken finally by a groan from Atterlothe.

"Of course, what a fool I have been. The Elizabeth Demdike puppet almost gave it away in Malkin Tower – what was it she said?" He cast his mind back for her exact words. "Ah yes, I remember.

A body that is neither human nor faery, that cannot die and needs no food. If taken care of, it could last forever

"She looked so greedy when she said it. Why did I not see?"

"I am to blame," said Aunt Salome. "To use the puppets was my idea. And it was I who woke the Old Ones to enlist their help. How they must have laughed at us."

"We could not have known," said Wayland Smith. "We did the best we could with the knowledge that we had. And the

Chattox and Demdike families, as well as our dear Mistress Alice, are safe in the Faery Realms."

"You are right, Wayland, of course," said Atterlothe. "The Old Ones will now hold the Glamour to the end. They wish to escape with their new bodies. They do not know of the letter, nor that we see their intentions. When all is done, we cut them down and destroy them. Only then will it be over."

The Silver Hare gave them all an unfathomable look with its moon bright eyes.

23. A HANGING AND AN EXPLOSION

On Thursday 20th August 1612, the good citizens of Lancaster prepared themselves for a large influx of visitors. Indeed, many had been arriving over the last two days. Taverns were full to bursting, and by noon many people were rather the worse for drink. Great crowds gathered outside the castle expectantly. The occasion was the day when, on Gallow's Hill, The Witches of Pendle were to hang from the neck until they were dead. A just punishment, it was believed.

Everyone was in gay attire, dressed in their Sunday best, for a hanging provided excellent entertainment. Today there were to be ten people hung all at once and each one a witch. The crowds couldn't believe their good fortune; it promised to be better than a coronation.

The castle gates opened and a great roar went up from the excited crowd. A procession of three horse drawn carts carried the prisoners and their coffins down the old Roman road through the centre of town. There they were, the Chattoxes, Demdikes and Mistress Nutter, each with their own secrets, along with a few unfortunates whom 'Jennet Demdike' in a fit of horrid expansiveness, had accused along with her own family.

The cheering crowd swarmed after them, pelting them merrily with rotten eggs and horse dung, yelling catcalls and obscenities. It was the most tremendous fun and all the street vendors were doing a roaring trade.

The procession stopped at the Golden Lion Inn, as was the custom, to allow the condemned a final drink. Anyone particularly observant might have noticed that the Chattoxes and Demdikes did not partake of this final comfort, and would perhaps have found it odd, but as most of the crowd were busily imbibing themselves, and were quite befuddled, it went largely unremarked.

Someone who did appear to be observant was a tall and broad man with a huge black beard. His keen eyes rarely left

183

the prisoners, and he took care not to let the jostling throng push him away from his vantage point close to the first cart. He was accompanied by a lad of about thirteen, well grown for his age, and like to be his son, a slender, cloaked man with bright green eyes who wore a broad- brimmed hat pulled down over his ears, and an unusual looking woman in gay clothes and gold hooped earrings. She had black hair and swarthy skin and might have been one of those travelling people who called themselves Egyptians. At last the carts were dragged with difficulty away from the inn and up the steep, rugged lane to Gallow's Hill.

It was a glorious day of blue sky and bright sunshine and the view was splendid. Morecombe Bay could be seen glittering in the far distance, if anyone had been interested. A small girl of about ten years old had positioned herself near to the gallows. She was slight, with green eyes, a pale face and a mass of wild red hair. She took no notice of anyone around her, and gazed at the platform, even though she was the object of much pointing and whispering.

"That's her, Jennet Demdike, the Witch's child."

"Aye, she's a cool one. She did denounce them all, her whole family, so they do say."

The black bearded man and his companions positioned themselves at various points around the scaffold.

The actual hangings were rather disappointing for the crowd as none of the prisoners screamed or howled or begged for mercy. Only James Demdike provided extra interest in that he appeared quite insensible and had to be held up by two men for the noose to be placed around his neck. However, all stayed until the bitter end, determined to wring every last drop of drama from the spectacle.

When the whole thing was over and the bodies of the condemned dangled quietly at the end of their ropes, swaying gently in the light breeze, the spectators began to disperse, trickling in groups down the hill and back, for the most part, to the Golden Lion. The black bearded man had a word with the executioner.

"I've come from the vicar of the parish of Newchurch. I'm the assistant sextant and I'm to take the bodies back for burial. I've got a cart with me."

The executioner had had enough of the whole affair by now; supper and a mug of ale were calling. Wayland Smith cut down the bodies of the Chattoxes, Demdikes and Mistress Nutter. Emmet and Atterlothe lifted them down into the coffins and loaded them onto the cart.

"Come Jennet," said Aunt Salome for the benefit of the last stragglers. "Let us take you home to your friends who will care for you now that your family is no more."

The Jennet puppet allowed herself to be lifted up beside Wayland Smith. Atterlothe, the Chovihani and Emmet climbed into the back of the cart and seated themselves firmly on the coffins. Pa clicked to the horse and they trundled their way homewards. No one spoke until they were some way out of the town and into the countryside when Master Smith turned to the Jennet puppet and said, "You spirits have played your part with great skill. The Company of the Silver Hare is grateful to you. I expect you long to return to the peace of the graveyard. We have kept you from it for a considerable while."

The Jennet puppet spoke in the voice of the youngest Old Demdike sister.

"I think you will find that only the Demdike Sisters are with you now. Mrs. Law and the others have already left the puppets they inhabited."

"Do not let us keep you," said the Elven King, politely. "You may now return whenever you wish. As Wayland Smith says, our Company is deeply indebted to you."

"Ah," returned the youngest Old Demdike, equally polite, "perhaps we are enjoying our foray into the world of the living too much to return. Perhaps we shall stay forever."

She raised her hand so that Wayland Smith saw her holding something small and bright. She leapt to her feet and hurled the object into the back of the cart. Atterlothe gave a warning shout but it was too late. There was a massive explosion, the old horse gave a horrible scream and the cart

was no more.

Emmet found himself in a muddy ditch. His ears were ringing and for a moment he had no idea what had happened. He heard his father's voice.

"Emmet, son, for pity's sake, answer me."

"I'm here Pa," Emmet called back feebly, and struggled out of the ditch.

Pa, Atterlothe and The Chovihani were standing in the lane looking dazed. Their faces were blackened and scorched, and Aunt Salome had a large cut on one cheek. The poor old horse had come off worst with a serious gash on its shoulder and was whimpering with fright and pain. The remains of the cart were strewn all over the road. The coffins had burst open to reveal the puppets, but those of Elizabeth, Alison and Jennet Demdike had vanished.

24. THE PARTING OF THE WAYS

"Magic used in conjunction with gunpowder - a deadly combination."

Wayland Smith spoke with a wry grimace.

The whole Company had gathered at the Faery Realms in Savine's outside room. The previous day had passed in a blur of activity. Atterlothe had healed and consoled the old carthorse who was wearing a nosebag liberally laced with Liquid Life Force. The cart had been repaired, the remaining puppets burnt and all the coffins, weighted with stones, buried on the north side of the graveyard.

Ma was worried by the excessive use of magic in broad daylight, but every precaution had been taken and as Atterlothe said, there had been no other way. Mistress Smith, weighed down by the anxiety and sorrow of the last few months, had given in willingly to the idea of rest and recuperation with her friends in the Faery Realms.

"But the no-time-at-all-has passed rule…" she began.

"…must apply," Atterlothe finished. "Trust me, it shall be so."

The reunion had been ecstatic. Lily flung herself on Jimmy and covered him with wet, sloppy kisses, and Henny Penny was happily reinstated under his arm, feathers sleek and glossy again, laying a large brown egg every few minutes.

Jennet and Emmet, after a swift, embarrassed hug were less effusive in their greeting, but the pink glow that surrounded them told a different story, and although they said little, they were always by each other's sides.

The Demdike family was saddened to hear of Old Demdike's fate in prison. Alison and Jennet wept inconsolably, but Elizabeth was more sanguine.

"My mother was a bitterly unhappy woman. The struggle between dark and light was always within her. At least her death was a useful one. And I am free of her," she added. "I have no love of magic, dark or light."

"What will you do now?" asked Mistress Alice. "I imagine you will not stay in the faery realms if you renounce magic, and you cannot return to Pendle."

"Mistress Chattox is tired of magic also. So be her daughter Lizzie. Alison and I will join them and open a tavern in the human realms, far away from Pendle." She thought for a moment and added, "A place where there be seafaring men."

"Why seafaring men?" Ma asked.

"Because," grinned Old Chattox, "they do like their drink, so it be told. And when they come ashore from a long voyage, they do have money in their pocket. Stands to reason it'll be drink as they will spend it on – our drink, if our hostelry be in the right place."

"We thought Portsmouth," said Alison. "We looked on the map. It is as far south as a body can get, right by the sea."

"You will need money for your scheme?" asked Mistress Alice.

"Nay," said Elizabeth, "Ma saved a lot over two hundred years. It be all hidden in the tower. Saved a fortune she did, and we all lived like the poorest of the poor. If someone could fetch it for us so as we can set up our tavern?"

"It shall be as you wish," said Atterlothe. "I think it is a good plan. I am sure your tavern will be a great success."

"What about Jimmy and Jennet?" said Ma.

"They will stay with me, I hope," said Mistress Alice looking questioningly at their mother.

"Aye, they were hardly my children anyway. My Ma took them over right from the start. Let them stay where they belong. Besides, my lass will marry your lad before many years are passed, if my eyes don't deceive me."

The Silver Hare had listened attentively and now spoke with its customary wisdom and grace.

"In our attempt to prevent a great evil from taking place in the world of men, we have woken an even greater evil. There is a lesson to be learned in all of this. Our actions can have unforeseen and far reaching effects, as we have witnessed to our cost. However, love, loyalty and friendship, these attributes abound in our beloved Company and all are of the light. Where these qualities thrive, no darkness can hold sway. Old Mistress Demdike left her dark path when she gave her life for True Love, redeeming herself. Her spirit can rest in peace."

Aunt Salome looked uneasy.

"Speak, my sister. What is on your mind?"

"What about the Old Ones, my Lord? They have escaped into the world of men. What shall be our course of action?"

"For now," said the Silver Hare in its starry voice, "I think we have acted enough. As a field lies fallow after harvest, so shall we rest for a while and gather our strength. The Old Ones will have to find somewhere to bide and create their life anew. We shall watch and wait. One day they will reveal themselves, and when they do we shall be ready. Until then, we will not trouble our minds with them. The great scales of the Universe hold darkness on one side, light on the other, never completely in balance as long as life endures."

Now that the adventures of the witch trials were behind them, the children were fully able to enjoy the Faery Realms. Speedwell took great delight in showing them many of the wondrous sights and they were enchanted. Pooka was almost fully grown now and would give all the children flights over the sea until Stella found out and put a stop to it.

"They are too heavy for you," she chided gently, "you will damage your wings."

Swimming with the mermaids was another favourite pastime, with the younger girls at least. The mermaids were stunningly beautiful, and friendly. As Atterlothe had foretold, they could not resist Emmet, swarming over him like bees around a honey pot, something which made poor Jennet so jealous that it took all Ma's efforts to make peace between them.

Delightful day followed delightful day and they did not want any of it to end, trying hard not to fear the future. But it

189

arrived, nevertheless. One evening, when they were all sitting around a fire in the orchard, The Chovihani announced that it was time for her people to move on.

"We have completed the task we came here to do. You have made us welcome, but traveling is in our blood. Tomorrow we shall be on our way."

"Dear Aunt Salome," the Elven Queen embraced her tenderly, "I shall miss you so much."

"And I you, but we will return. Always we will return."

Mistress Alice arose from her seat by the Chovihani.

"And I shall go with them."

"But Mistress Alice," said Atterlothe, "we thought you would remain here with us. You are so beloved by our family."

"I know, and I am grateful to you both, but I am not of the Faery Folk and my place is in the human world. I could not settle here. But I shall not be alone – my beloved Anne will accompany me. I hope that you all understand and will not be offended."

Anne Chattox stood up and slipped her arm through that of her Mistress.

"How could you ever cause offence to anyone?"

"We shall travel in disguise and re-invent ourselves," she said, kissing Mistress Alice's cheek. "It will be an adventure. Who knows, we may even get to Portsmouth and visit my Ma's tavern.

"Jimmy and Jennet," asked Mistress Alice, "will you come with us?"

Silence. Emmet's heart was beating so loudly he felt everyone must hear it. Jimmy answered for them both.

"My Jimmy and my Jennet will come," he said, "and Henny Penny."

Jennet jumped up, knocking over the stool she was seated on, and ran from the fire into the darkness. Emmet followed, stumbling and tripping over obstacles.

"Jennet, wait."

He found her where he knew he would, at the place where the green meadowland gave way to sand, just above the sea.

She sat looking out into darkness, tears rolling down her cheeks. He sat beside her and put his arms around her, too shaken to be shy.

"You are going away with the Egyptians?" Her face wore the look he knew so well. "But Jennet, why? I thought you and I, well, we…"

"Jimmy can't come back," said Jennet, "everyone thinks he was hanged and I can't abandon him. Besides, I would be hated for denouncing the others. They would never let me forget it. It would be unbearable."

"But you could stay with Speedwell," said Emmet. "I could visit you."

"Emmet," Jennet disentangled herself from his arms and took his hand, "it isn't our time, not yet. We must grow up first. You are one of the Chosen, you need to finish your training with Pooka, finish learning how to be a blacksmith. I can't just sit and wait. I want to do things, too."

They sat silently hand in hand, watching the silvery patterns that the bright moon made on the sea. Emmet could feel the cold, hollow feeling coming back into his chest. He realised that he would have to get used to it being there.

"I will come back though," said Jennet, "and if we need each other, we can use the silver amulets."

Emmet looked at her in surprise. "How do you mean?"

Jennet gave him her most beautiful smile.

"Don't forget," she said, "in times of trouble, they will always bring us home. Home is where the heart is, and my heart is with you, your heart is with me. The amulet will do the rest."

The next day, the Egyptians dismantled their beautiful tents and loaded everything onto their horses and donkeys. The Elven King and Queen presented Mistress Alice with a farewell present, a brightly painted cart with a wooden house on top. It had a door at the front and two tiny windows. Inside was a large fitted bed for the women and Jennet, and behind a curtain, a pull-out bunk for Jimmy. There were fitted shelves, cupboards and a stove the like of which no one had ever seen before.

"It's wonderful," Mistress Smith was quite overwhelmed.

"Not quite Roughlee Hall," said Atterlothe, "but it is a step up from a tent. I mean no offence, Obadiah," he added hastily, for the old master carver had come to have a closer look.

"None taken, Your Highness, but this has given me ideas. Yes, indeed. Markus, stir your lazy carcass lad and come take a look at this contraption."

Aunt Salome said, "Atterlothe, you may just have changed the way these Egyptians live. I have never seen Obadiah so excited."

There was much embracing and weeping from Lily who not only was heartbroken at the idea of losing Jimmy but wanted desperately to live in the beautiful cart.

"Why can't I go too, Ma? Oh, please let me go too."

"There is not room in the bed, Lily," said Anne, tactfully. "But I am sure one day you could pay us a visit."

A hundred conversations took place, there was so much for so many to say, but perhaps the most important was between Emmet and Jennet when they spoke again a while later. Emmet took Jennet to one side. "It's alright," he said, "I've been thinking about everything and I know that you are right. But I still need to ask you something now," and he fished inside his scrip. "When we are older," he said, "when you are ready, will you marry me?"

She stared at him for a long moment, and her green eyes were bright with tears.

"Of course, I will, Emmet, you know I will."

"Give me your hand, then."

Emmet slipped a simple silver ring onto her finger. As he did so, the universe quickly turned inside out and back again. He looked around nervously, afraid something was coming to change this moment, but Jennet was beaming through her tears.

"It was my wish," she said. "Remember the wishes that

the Silver Hare gave us? My wish has come true."

Emmet was bewildered. "You wished we would get married? But you'd only just met me."

"No silly, not that. I wished that I could belong to your family for ever and ever."

They were ready to leave and the procession of horses and the bright coloured cart began to wend their way out of the orchard. All goodbyes had been said. The Smiths and the Royal Family watched until they were out of sight.

"Dry your eyes, Lily," said Ma, "we shall see them all at Halloween."

"Halloween?" asked Emmet.

"Of course," said Atterlothe. "Ma Demdike's spirit will be coming up for the first time. There will be a big celebration for her. All that are left of the Company will be there. And you, Emmet, will have an important part to play."

25. FAREWELL TO MISTRESS DEMDIKE

A silvery mist hung over the graveyard. The full moon lit up the droplets of moisture on the cobwebs like faery lanterns, creating a festive air. The Spirits of the Dead had arisen from their resting places and joined with the Company of the Silver Hare. All formed a group on the north side of the graveyard. The faery musicians played a lilting tune. Savine and Speedwell, who normally never left the Faery Realms, were there, and Emmet mounted proudly on Pooka. All eyes were on a small mound of brown earth with no stone or cross to mark it. A wispy form began to emerge, the skinny, scowling form of Old Demdike. The musicians stopped playing and a great cheer went up, loud enough to wake the dead, if they hadn't been awake already.

"Mistress Demdike, hurrah!"

She gazed about and then looked at her ghostly hands.

"So, I be dead then? Well, I never!" A sudden look of panic passed over her wasted features. "The Old Ones, where are they? Did you find my liquid letter?"

The Silver Hare spoke tenderly in its starry voice.

"All is well, my sister. Everything you set out to do has been accomplished, have no fear."

It was a wonderful party. Aunt Salome, Mistress Alice, Jimmy and Jennet all returned. Jennet had grown taller over the last months, and as she danced with Emmet, the moonlight glinting on her silver ring, he thought that perhaps being grown up didn't seem so far away, after all.

The night wore on until, at a sign from the Silver Hare, Figwort blew loudly on his trumpet and silence fell. Everyone stopped dancing and gathered around.

"Dear friends, we are here tonight to welcome the Spirit of our dear sister, Mistress Demdike."

Here there were more hurrahs. The Silver Hare held up its paw and the cheers died away.

"We are here both to welcome her and to bid her farewell.

She gave her life willingly to save the Company, even in the belief that the Old Ones would torment her spirit throughout all eternity. She died a heroine, all stains of blackness wiped from her soul. Therefore, her spirit may go straight to Paradise, to the arms of the Great Mother. Emmet and Pooka, step forward, please."

The throng of Spirits and living parted to allow them through, Emmet already mounted on the back of the Faery horse who high stepped up to the Silver Hare.

"Pooka's name," it went on, "means Spirit Horse, whose task is to carry dead heroes to Paradise. Emmet and Pooka, escorting Mistress Demdike's spirit will be your first task as a Chosen Pair. Are you ready?"

Emmet raised his fist in the air in salute and Pooka whinnied, "We are."

The Silver Hare looked at the tattered grey spirit kindly with its moon bright eyes.

"Mistress, one of your kin may accompany you on your last journey, as far as the gates. Who shall it be?"

"Jennet," said Old Demdike without hesitation, "my Scarlet Flower."

"Then my sister, go in peace."

Pooka flew higher and higher through the night sky, past constellations new and strange. Emmet sat in front, holding onto her silver mane with Jennet behind clinging to his waist and the weightless wraith of old Demdike resting beside them in the hollow of one of Pooka's wings, holding Jennet's arm.

"How do we know where to go?" asked Jennet. "Where is Paradise?"

"Look out for a constellation shaped like a hare," said Emmet. "When we find it, we must use the naming gift that the Horned Hunter gave us."

He took one hand from Pooka's mane and patted a leather bag that hung from his waist. Jennet opened it carefully and took out a small silver trumpet, curiously engraved, on a silken cord. She placed it around Emmet's neck.

195

"There," cried the spirit of Old Demdike, pointing, "over to the right, that's it!"

The constellation glittered in the velvety blackness. Emmet put the silver trumpet to his lips and blew a long blast. For a moment all remained silent, then faintly, in the distance, they heard the now familiar ghostly baying of hounds.

THE END

THE PENDLE WITCH TRIALS

The Pendle Witch Trials of 1612 were set against a background of superstition, fear and lawlessness.

Two families living on Pendleside, each headed by an elderly matriarch, those of Chattox and Demdike, were accused, along with the lady of the manor, Mistress Alice Nutter.

The magistrate, Alice Nutter's neighbour Roger Nowell, had been in a bitter dispute with her over her land the previous year which he had lost at some financial cost; perhaps he saw this as a chance to take revenge.

All were tried, incarcerated in Lancaster Gaol and hanged, largely denounced by Jennet Demdike, daughter and granddaughter of two of the accused. She was only nine years old. Her brother James was said to be half-witted and became so ill with fear in prison that he had to be carried unconscious to be hung.

What would make a child denounce her entire family and send them to their deaths?

I have woven a fantasy around these figures of history to try to give them a happier outcome.

I am always on the side of the witches...

Joy Pitt, 2018

ABOUT THE AUTHOR

Joy Pitt is a professional storyteller and puppeteer in the oral tradition.

When she isn't busy storytelling in schools, festivals and libraries, Joy spends her time painting and writing. Home is a small, dusty cottage on the edge of the Lincolnshire Wolds where she lives with her husband, who is a woodcutter, and a bad-tempered cat called Annabelle.

Joy has three children who have gone out into the world to seek their fortune.

This is her first book.